A DEMON AND HER SCOT

WELCOME TO HELL #4

EVE LANGLAIS

Copyright © July 2013, Eve Langlais

Cover Art by Dreams2Media July 2017

Produced in Canada

Published by Eve Langlais

KDP ISBN: 978-1492108382

E-ISBN: 978-1-927459-40-9

INGRAM ISBN: 978-1-988328-74-4

PROLOGUE

SCONCES IGNITED as the devil's irritation overflowed and manifested itself in the form of flames. Usually, he held better control over his power; however, the golf tourney loomed only days away, and Lucifer still hadn't figured out how he'd cheat his way to victory.

"There's got to be a way," he mumbled as he paced his living room—decorated in the latest fashion, or so the demon he'd hired from Hell's Home Design claimed. A chimera shag rug, whose plush lion and goat fur contrasted nicely with the smooth snakeskin texture, tickled his bare cloven feet. A floor-to-ceiling volcanic rock fireplace of the deepest ebony, which blazed to life as his gaze lit upon it. A sectional sofa covered in troll leather, the skin worked until it was as soft as a demon baby's ass. Oh and a ninety-inch Sharp Aquos, a television made for a man and his action movies, the stunning sound and picture quality so vivid, so real, it was almost like being there in person.

The fact it currently displayed some wimpy-looking guy bent in a pretzel failed to send him on a rant, just like his on again-off again paramour, bent over in spandex doing yoga, couldn't distract him from his dilemma.

As if noticing his lack of commentary on her posterior, Gaia peeked at him upside down from between her legs and queried, "A way to do what?"

"Win."

"Are we talking war or that bloody golf match?"

"That bloody golf match is a war! A war to see who is the best." Usually a foregone conclusion as far as he was concerned, however, given the competition he'd face this time round, not a sure thing, or so his psychics claimed. *Intolerable.*

"It's just a game."

"Wh-what!" He sputtered the word and halted his pacing. "Just a game, she says? Have you not paid attention? We are talking about the most powerful beings in the universe, coming together for a once-in-every-century event, an event viewed by zillions."

"I've been paying attention. How could I not? You've only been running commercials about it every two minutes on HBC." Hell's Broadcasting Corporation, the only channel to watch in the pit, other than PBS, which was reserved for inmates as its own special form of torture. "I, for one, am dying to see a bunch of males with nothing better to do with their time and power than hit a little ball with L-shaped sticks." Her dry tone smacked of mockery.

"You have no respect," he muttered with disgust.

"Nope. None at all," she admitted with a wink. "Want

to punish me for it?" She waggled her ass suggestively. For a moment, he toyed with the idea of giving her the punishment she demanded. But then he thought of his latest spy reports claiming his brother, who liked to call himself the Almighty One, had improved his game by over five strokes! And all because of a new caddy, one he'd not yet managed to steal or destroy.

"I need a teacher."

Gaia almost landed on her head, the shock of his admission obviously unbalancing her. He knew the feeling. It stuck in his craw to admit he required help.

"Holy buzzing bees," she exclaimed. "You? Taking lessons?" She chortled. "Oh, that I'd pay to see."

His dark glare, which had frightened countless over the centuries, did nothing but make her laugh louder. "I fail to see the humor."

"Says the demon who is usually such a know-it-all."

"Knowing it all hasn't helped my swing, though." He couldn't intimidate the dimpled golf ball into heading straight to the hole. He knew this firsthand, having tried it.

"And just who do you trust to give you advice? Or more accurately, who is left? If I remember correctly, you tossed anyone who ever beat you at the game into the abyss for recycling."

He had. Lucifer couldn't abide people with natural talent, and he hated to lose. "There is one guy I've left alone."

"Who?"

"A certain Scot."

Her eyes widened. "Him? But he swore he'd never play again."

"He also swore he'd never fall prey to a woman's wiles again."

"He hasn't."

"Yet."

A gasp left his lover. "Oh no. Are you still playing matchmaker?"

"Who said I ever stopped? I've got a knack for it if I say so myself. I went through my employee files and came across the perfect candidate for that ornery Scot. It's time a certain slithery minion of mine did her duty to my empire."

"But with him? They'll hate each other."

"I know. Won't it be fun to watch?" As his plan fermented, so did his ardor finally rise to a boil. Nothing like multitasking—AKA plotting evil at the detriment of others for his amusement and gain to get the blood flowing, which, in turn, would get his sassy girlfriend doing something more productive with her mouth than talking.

As usual, it was great being the Lord of Sin.

1

"I NEED you to find me a Scot."

Sharpening the edge of her battle-axe while sitting on a rock at the edge of the training grounds, Aella held in a sigh. Not another stupid task. The sweat still cooled on her body from her recent workout—where she'd kicked some cocky demon ass around the training ring. She'd looked forward to a long, hot soak—with frothy bubbles, of course—followed by an evening of doing nothing but playing Candy Crush—level sixty-five had her stumped. Recognizing the voice, though, she knew better than to ignore the speaker, no matter how strange the request. Why did her boss want a fancy tie? "You want me to find an ascot? Didn't those go out of style a few centuries ago?"

Brows beetling together, the distinguished gent with silver at his temples, dressed in a sharply pressed Armani suit with wing-tipped polished loafers, known as the Lord of Sin, Beelzebub, or more commonly as Satan, frowned.

Not an I'm-about-to-make-you-wish-you'd-never-crossed-my-path grimace, more of a what-the-fuck-do-you-mean? "No, I don't want an ascot. I need a Scot, as in a man dressed in a kilt."

Still just as odd, but hey, he signed her paycheck. "Skirt-wearing man. Gotcha." Aella tested the edge of her weapon—the bead of blood welling on the tip of her finger attested to its sharpness—before she slid her dusty, booted feet off the massive rock where she'd propped them. "I'll get right on it, boss." She knew of a few bars not far from here that catered to men who liked to wear frilly things.

"Slow down a second. I'm not done giving you the details. See, I don't want just any man in a kilt. You need to fetch me Niall McGregor."

The name didn't ring any bells. "Any particular reason why?"

"Why? Don't you watch sports at all? Niall McGregor is only the greatest golfer who ever lived. Or he used to be. Damned man gave it up centuries ago over a silly misunderstanding."

Hmm, knowing her lord, she doubted it was as minor as he indicated. "Why do I get the impression there's more to that story?"

"Because there is."

"Anything I need to know?"

With a vague wave, Lucifer replied, "Nothing pertinent to your mission. Suffice it to say the Scot hasn't lifted a club since the incident. Such a waste of talent."

Even more curious now, she had to ask, "If he's retired, then what do you need him for?"

"To caddy for me, of course, in the upcoming tournament, Golf Across the Planes. It only happens once every hundred years and is quite the event. Surely you've heard of it. It's being advertised every few minutes on HBC."

Yeah, she'd seen it, and fast forwarded the commercials, which featured everyone's favorite devil. Check any dictionary in Hell and under the definition of attention whore was an image of her boss. If he wasn't the center of attention, then he was killing or torturing whoever was. "Oh, that tournament. Already got my DVR set, boss, so I don't miss a minute." Everyone who intended to keep a head on their shoulders did. Or at least lied about it. Some might sneer at ass-kissing, but Aella credited it with buying her big screen television and her cool new pump-action shotgun with the spattering acid pellets. "I gotta ask, if this Scot of yours hasn't lifted a club in centuries, how do you figure he'll help you?"

"A talent like that never completely vanishes. Once a great golfer, always a great golfer."

Her turn to raise a brow. "Really? Has anyone told Tiger Woods that?"

Withholding a smirk, Aella watched the smoke curl from her lord's ears. So easy to rile, yet, despite his temper, Lucifer was a decent employer. Of all the people, demons, and other entities she'd dealt with over the centuries since her descent to Hell, Satan, in an odd twist, proved the fairest. And the most fun to antagonize, once you learned to dodge his groping hands.

Lucifer scowled. "Don't talk to me about Tiger. He made a deal with the wrong god." In other words, someone other than Lucifer. "Him and his stupid morals. You'd think these famous types would know better than to try and hold onto their souls. Don't most of them realize I'll own them in the end anyway?"

Ah yes, because Heaven's requirements to pass its pearly gates kept getting more and more complicated. "Any idea where I can find this paragon of dimpled white balls?"

"How the fuck should I know? It's why I'm giving the job to you. But, if I were to guess, I'd wager he's getting drunk somewhere in a bar."

She couldn't help bugging him a little. Her payback for not getting her planned evening of relaxation. "You mean you don't know where he is? I thought you owned his soul."

"I do, but you try keeping track of billions of damned souls, demons, and other little fuckers who seem to think they can just move whenever and where they like in the nine circles and not leave a forwarding address with the census bureau."

"Maybe if you hadn't outsourced it to some call center with customer service reps who only speak dead languages, your ability to locate them would work better. No one can understand a blasted thing they say."

Not at all offended at her criticism, Lucifer grinned. "Which is what makes it so much fun. Now stop questioning me. I am lord of this realm, and I command you to do my bidding. As a hunter in my employ, it's your job to find things. So find him. And quickly too. The match is only days away."

"If you need him so bad, then why did you wait so

long?" Impertinence ever was a failing of hers. Thankfully, Lucifer didn't see it as a flaw. Most of the time.

"My last prospect had an unfortunate accident."

"I hardly call throwing your latest golf instructor into the abyss an accident."

"Heard about that, did you?"

"Heard? It was all over Helltube. Do you know his scream of descent is the longest recorded one at forty-six hours, seven minutes?"

"The man had good lungs. Pity he couldn't teach worth a shit."

Pity her lord couldn't golf worth a damn, not that anyone dared tell him. Lucifer might love the game of golf, but the sport certainly didn't love him back. The only reason he ever came close to winning was because he cheated. Or killed the competition. In the case of his match every century against his brother God and other powerful beings, thankfully, they were all just as bad.

Horrible players or not, everyone still watched the televised event. To not cheer their lord was the surest way to draw his formidable ire. Beside, the entertainment value couldn't be beat.

With only the vaguest of information, AKA a name, Aella left the training grounds and Lucifer—who, swinging his mighty black sword, bellowed for someone to come and play with him. She wondered which unlucky demon would end up with the short straw. Depending on the boss's mood, sparring could end up bringing glory and a spot with Lucifer's elite guard, or death. Gambling with their lives wasn't high on any demon's list.

With no idea where to start, Aella headed for the shop

of her favorite and most accurate psychic. In the mortal realm, magic existed in weak amounts, and charlatans claiming special powers abounded. However, in Hell, the esoteric forces ran strong. Demons and other entities with abilities to conjure, locate, and shape those forces were common, if for the most part short-lived. The competition amongst practitioners was fierce, but if you could find a good one, handy for a hunter like herself.

Calling a portal, her own magic abundant enough to sketch a one-woman doorway to places she'd visited before, Aella exited right outside the shop in the third circle of the pit. The flashing neon of the sign in the window promised, *Fortunes, Curses, and the Best Souvlaki.* Seriously. No one could beat Sasha's blend of herbs on the mystery meat she called pork, although rumor said this part of the neighborhood had a lower number of hellrats than other areas. Whatever she used, it tasted damned good over a bed of rice with a Greek salad and tzitziki sauce.

Aella strode in to the discordant clanging of a handful of bells strung over the door. Within the shop, the familiar scent of roasting meat and fragrant herbs tickled her nose. Murky due to the ash-stained window and the single hanging light draped in colored crystals, Aella peered toward the back, seeking her friend. "Sasha? You working today? I need your help to find someone."

From the rear of the room, a beaded curtain rustled as her friend made her appearance. Most people expected a wizened old woman, heavily draped in veils and scarves with large hoop earrings. Talk about a stereotype. Sasha was more of a modern gypsy sporting the most disreputable mini skirt possible, a crop top showing off her naval piercing, and short, spiked hair currently colored a fiery red. Aella thought her nasal piercing of a unicorn was a particularly nice touch.

"Aella! My favorite bitch. I haven't seen you in ages."

"Sorry. I've been busy working for the big guy. Lots of misbehaving demons and souls lately."

"Tell me about it. The forces that be have been driving me nuts with their omens and shit."

"Oh. What have they been saying?" Unlike some crazies, when Sasha claimed spirits spoke to her, she meant it. Sasha compared it to being a conduit for any deity too cheap to take an ad out in the *New Hell Times*.

Eyes rolling up until only the whites showed, Sasha slipped into freaky mode. A deep voice emerged from her hot-pink-painted lips. "The time comes when the great and powerful Lord of Sin shall once again show his true worth, and all will tremble before his might and join him in the battle."

Hot as Hell or not, Aella still felt a shiver. She hated fucked-up premonition shit like this.

Sasha's eyes returned to normal, and she smiled. "Ha, what do you know? Sounds like Satan's about to lay a smackdown on his minions. About time. Some of the folk are getting brazen even for Hell. But that's not why you're here. You're looking for a hunky Scot."

Knowing better than to question her friend's knowledge, Aella nodded. "Yup. Some dude called Niall McGregor. Any idea where he is?"

"Of course. He hasn't budged in a few decades. You'll find him at the Triple D."

Aella's nose wrinkled. "Ugh. Not that hole. Hasn't someone bombed the place yet?" Nothing short of an incinerating blast would ever remove the stain of despair from that dump.

Despite the human media's portrayal, Hell wasn't that much different from the mortal realm. If one could ignore the reddish cast to the sunless sky, the constantly sifting ash, and the general air of melancholy, the pit looked like hundreds of other industrialized cities. Big buildings, many in need of repair. Crowded streets. Pitted roads. How bad depended on the location. The inner ring where Lucifer resided in his massive castle was the most up kept; the mansions lavish, the streets mostly cobbled, the air fresher, the crowding and corruption not so prevalent. The farther out one went, the less civilized things got, the more the buildings fell into disrepair, the rougher and less interested in maintaining the infrastructure the populace got. Aella lived in the fourth ring, the best she could afford. Sasha's shop resided in the third.

With that said, the only exception to the ring rule was the area around the abyss. Located via a winding road whose origin was lost to the sands of time—and swallowed by the giant, myopic serpent that lived in that desolate desert—the abyss was literally a giant hole in the center of Hell. Kind of the Grand Canyon of the pit and the place souls went when they'd paid their penance and wanted to move on. Lucifer liked to call it the minion recycler. The damned ones called it their second chance. It was the most feared and, at the same time, most revered location in Hell.

You'd think the opportunity to live again, to live a

good and righteous life that might send a reborn soul to Heaven during their next round, would see the damned ones lining up to throw themselves in. On the contrary, it often took centuries, sometimes longer, for most to take the plunge. Something about truly dying, having their memories and their souls wiped clean, scared the fuck out of them. It was that fear that made the area surrounding the abyss such a miserable zone. Those who wanted the rebirth felt drawn, but lacking the courage, they lingered. They drank. They pondered. They hesitated. As a result, the area turned into a dump. People on the verge of suicide didn't care if the roof collapsed around their heads or if the dust grew thick enough to act as a mattress.

Fuck did Aella hate visiting that depressing place. As a demon, Aella would never end up using the abyss, unless she wanted a permanent death. Demons didn't have souls like humans. Once they died, they were gone for good.

Good thing she'd proven too tough to kill—and that she kissed great ass. Lucifer had his favorite minions spelled to make them practically immortal. A handy tool to have when he needed to punish. After all, it was hard to flay the skin from a naughty soul eternally when they croaked within minutes from blood loss.

"Got time for a cup of coffee?" Sasha asked.

"I really should get going. Lucifer needs this Scot as soon as possible. Upcoming golf tourney, you know."

"Oh I know. It's going to be a doozy too."

If Sasha said so, then she knew it was true. "Any hints on the winner?"

"The future is still unclear. The paths still split."

"You suck. My bookie is waiting for me to lay a bet, but I'm still hedging on who to put my money on."

"Fuck the dog."

"What?"

"Hellhound racing. Saturday's match. Fuck the Dog is a sure win, if his trainer doesn't get caught by his wife screwing his girlfriend while using baby oil on satin sheets."

"That is way too much information."

"Tell me about it. I got a peek of it in living color, and trust me when I say that trainer naked isn't something anyone wants to see."

"Can I take a rain check on the coffee?"

"Of course. You'll be back soon enough."

"I will?"

"Yup. Oh, and the answer is forever."

"Answer to what?"

"I can't tell you the question yet. It's in the future. But, since you're such a stubborn bitch, I thought I'd help you with the answer."

"I hate it when you do that," Aella grumbled.

"I know." Sasha smiled smugly. "Here's lunch to go." Sasha handed her a paper bag, which magically appeared at her elbow.

Aella's stomach gurgled. She didn't need psychic powers to know what hid within would taste good. Damned good. "Thanks. Hey, before I go, how's the romance coming with that vampire, what's his name?"

"Vlad? I staked him. He was going to cheat on me and break my heart." Sasha shrugged. "I broke his first."

Never screw around with a psychic. Especially not

murderous ones. After hugging goodbye and promising to get together soon, Aella left. As she munched her souvlaki right off the stick, she couldn't help mull Sasha's mysterious words. Forever. *What the fuck does that mean?*

And even more perplexing, what was the damned question?

2

EVEN THROUGH THE hank of stringy hair hanging over his eyes, McGregor noted her the moment she strode in. Everyone with a cock did. It was not often a female such as her tarnished her reputation by entering this bar. Only those who'd lost all hope ever came here. Dirty, dank, and disreputable, the Triple D—Despair, Desperation, and Destiny— catered to those one step away from flinging themselves in the abyss. They charged too much for the drinks, astronomical prices for their whores, and encouraged those who entered to wager their every last penny before they went on to the next stage of their unlife. Or, as some called it, their rebirth.

Hell, despite what many believed, wasn't the final stop when a soul died, more of a way station, a place of judgment for sins. Once a soul paid for their misdeeds when they lived, they could choose to eke out an existence in the overcrowded cities that littered the nine rings or take their chance with the abyss and start over. Wipe the slate clean so to speak.

Problem was, no one was quite sure what that meant. People who entered the abyss didn't return. Or, at least, their memories didn't. Once their souls got recycled, hopefully to end up reborn, no one ever heard from them again.

Needless to say, this uncertainty led to many choosing to delay their final plunge to the next level. As a result? Hell was a crowded fucking place.

Except for here, at the edge of the abyss. Here, the damned didn't choose to set down roots. So close to this major landmark, only a few dared to set up shop and eke out a living. The very lack of crowds and the general air of misery was why McGregor chose it. He enjoyed the quiet, the solitude, the chance to stagnate in misery. Oh, and the ale was wonderfully strong, if you had the coin to pay for it, and thanks to his deal with the devil, Niall had plenty of that.

He could have anything he wanted. Whores? The only other thing of worth in this place, if you could call the blood-sucking slags in this place by such a kind name, abounded. They could make quite the profit selling their charms to those determined to spend it all before going away. Not that Niall paid the slags any mind. He'd stopped partaking of their services a few centuries ago. Why have meaningless sex? Fuck one, you'd fucked them all. Once he lost interest, though, it became a game with the sex workers. Try and seduce the Scot. See what he wore under his kilt. He bore it with good grace most days.

On those he didn't...he always paid for his damages.

Niall had no interest in pleasure. He lived, if you could call it that, for the next drink. And even that he cared very little about. He'd gone through all the stages that resulted in an acceptance of his fate.

Stage One. Rage and revenge. Done during his mortal years, he didn't recall much other than the fact rinsing with cold water didn't always wash away the bloodstains.

Stage Two. A twinge of remorse. Not much mind you, but once the battles were done and the dust settled, he discovered the pain at the treachery done him unabated. All that bloodshed. Comrades lost. People reviling his name. And yet, he still couldn't forget…

Stage Three. Depression. Owning the title to all kinds of land did him no good when no one would marry him. Sure, the lairds of other castles promised him daughters—who wouldn't when they feared retaliation?—but none of the women wanted him. None wanted the Fearsome McGregor who chopped off his first bride's head and drank her blood. He didn't—the blood drinking came later—but legend was a powerful thing.

Stage Four. Death. When the last keep he conquered rebelled in the middle of the night, he lay in bed and waited for the assassination. Even looked his killer in the frightened whites of his eyes and muttered a thank you. He was done living. He longed for death and an end to the emptiness in his heart. Problem was he woke up, in Hell, which, as it turned out, was just as annoying as the mortal world.

Stage Five. Bitterness, which led to Stage Six, drunkenness. Because of his deal with Lucifer, he didn't own his soul, so he couldn't just jump in to the abyss and start over. Despite Niall's many wars and crimes, he didn't receive punishment. On the contrary, Lucifer gave him a medal for sending so many deserving souls his way.

Oh, and he became a vampire. Apparently, those without a soul entering the pit only had a few choices. Become a demon of some sort or a type of undead. Since he preferred to not turn into a creature of nightmare, Niall chose the existence of a blood-sucking, sun-hating vampire. It went well with his mood.

As for the next stages of his fate? Niall couldn't name them, nor did he care. He just waited for his miserable existence to end. Or for Hell to freeze over so he could try out that new mortal sport he'd seen on television called hockey. And that was his life, in a bleak, shriveled nutshell. Boring. Depressing. Monotonous. Until *she* walked in.

What set her apart?

Everything.

Good-looking, a real model-type lady—a term he didn't use often—she definitely made an impression in her mottled snake skin, thigh-high boots, off-the-shoulder red toga and dark hair drawn back and held high in a swinging pony tail—made for yanking as a male pounded into her from behind. She exuded a cockiness better suited to a man and the sensuality of a high-priced whore. A heady combination. However, it was the double-edged axe strapped to her back, the leather harness accentuating a plentiful bosom, that really intrigued him.

As she questioned the barkeep, he eyed her, wondering if she could wield the monstrous weapon or if it acted as a prop, a way of dissuading the more gullible into thinking she was tough. Judging by her build, sinuous curves, and undulating hips, he would wager against. Pretty girls, such as her, had other weapons in their arsenal.

Interest from all the patrons, himself included, was piqued when the barkeep inclined his head in Niall's direction, and she spun to fix him with striking orbs, yellow and vertically slitted, much like a cat. Her full lips pursed as she eyed him. Never one to shy away from bold gazes, Niall leaned back in his rickety seat, spread his legs slightly so his tartan pulled taut across his thick bare legs, and waited for her to approach. When she seemed to hesitate, he patted his lap, curious to see how far this female would go to earn a few coins. She'd not come here because she'd heard he was attractive. Then again, paid by the hour, women of her ilk didn't care about looks but the size of his purse. Until they saw the size of his cock. Then they demanded more—of his cock that was, not his money.

With a sure stride, she weaved her way through the rickety furniture until she stood before his table. Still staring, she didn't say a word. Surely she didn't expect him to ask for it? She wanted him; she could damned well beg for it.

They engaged in a staring match, neither of them blinking. A stalemate. Bored, he belched. Her eyes narrowed, the pupils dilating to a mere black slit, and she crossed her arms under her impressive chest. He almost asked her to bare them so he could take a peek at her merchandise, but that would indicate interest, and Niall had more willpower than that.

The silence stretched as she again eyeballed him from

the top of his shaggy head, down his untrimmed beard, over his stained tunic, to his ragged plaid, and then farther, right to the tip of his dirty bare toes. What a sight he must have presented. He'd not bathed or groomed in a decade or two. Maybe three. He'd lost count.

"You have got to be fucking kidding me," she muttered at last.

Such foul language from such pretty lips. He rather enjoyed it. "Excuse me, lass, ye seem a tad lost. Were ye looking for someone?"

"Are you Niall McGregor?"

Oh ho. The plot thickened. Few knew him by name. Generally referred to as the Scot, Niall hadn't heard his name spoken in at least a century or more. Someone obviously had sent her searching for him. But who? He'd eschewed those he knew in life, preferring to marinate in his self-inflicted misery. Most who'd once known him had moved on, their souls not fettered by a covenant signed in blood, a contract damning him to the pit forever—and giving him a thirst for more than just ale. "Aye, I'm he."

"*The* Niall McGregor?"

"Depends. Who's asking?"

"I am unfortunately." She didn't bother to stop her lip from curling into a moue of disgust.

Shame at his appearance fought to rise. He booted it back down. What did he care what she thought of him? Best find out what she wanted—*my cock is hers for the asking*—and send her on her way. "What can I do for ye, lass?" The endearment slipped out, a habit from his more civilized days. Funny. He could have sworn he didn't have any civility left in him.

"Not me. Our lord. Lucifer wants your ragged ass back at his castle pronto."

Her answer surprised him. "For?"

"He requires your assistance with his upcoming golf match."

For a moment, Niall recalled the thrill of holding a club in his hand. Of lining up the perfect shot. The sound the head made when it hit the ball's sweet spot. Then, with even greater clarity, he recalled what golf did to him. "No."

"What do you mean no?"

"I mean no. I am not going back to Lucifer's castle. I'm no longer in the golfing game. So march your sweet buttocks back to him and tell him you found me, but the answer is no."

How he enjoyed the flummoxed mien on her face. "You do realize he's the boss?"

"I know and don't care. What's he going to do to me? Sentence me to Hell? Already there, lass."

"He could make your stay a lot more unpleasant."

"How? I've done my share of pain. Shed my pints of blood. Tried just about every torture this damned place has to offer." Anything to try and *feel* again. None of it worked. Niall rolled his shoulders in a shrug. "He's welcome to do his worst. I dinna feel a thing." His brogue thickened with his irritation.

The answer thinned those plump lips into a straight line. Sour mood or not, she was still too damned attractive, and worse, the longer she stayed, the more she drew attention. From the dark corners, shadows—which had lain dormant for many, many years—crept forward, drawn by her feisty spirit. If she didn't leave, she'd soon discover why the brighter souls and demons chose to avoid this place.

Just like many a female with a one-track mind, she seemed oblivious to the approaching menace. "Are we going to do this the easy way or the hard?" she asked. "Because, like it or not, you will be coming with me. I've got an impeccable record when it comes to completing my missions, and I am not giving up the title or my bonus just because some ancient, hairy caveman—"

He took offense at the insult. "I'm a Scot!"

"—refuses to get his fat ass—"

"Fat?" He straightened from his slouch to glare at her. "I'll have you know, this is all muscle, lass."

"—out of his chair and toddle his skirted, dirty self to the nearest fucking portal."

"Anyone ever tell you that you have a foul mouth?"

The dirty mouth in question curled into a derisive smile. "All the time. It's one of my more endearing qualities. So, what's it going to be, Nancy?"

His brows drew together in a fierce frown that didn't daunt her one bit. "My name is Niall. And the answer is still no. I am not budging."

"Listen, Nellie. I am going to be nice here, given Lucifer did ask me to bring you to him with as little damage as possible, but you are trying my nonexistent patience. Don't make me hurt you. I can promise you won't like it."

As if this sweet little thing could harm him. He did, however, find her attitude perplexing. "What is up with name calling, lassie?"

"It's the skirt. It's throwing me off."

"It's a kilt."

"Whatever. Kilt, skirt. You're still a man showing off his bare legs in something that went out of style centuries ago."

"Says the girl wearing a toga."

"If it's any consolation, I'd make fun of a male, even a Greek, wearing one of those too."

Niall changed tactics. With a leer, he asked, "So what are you wearing under it?"

She tossed it right back at him. "What are you wearing under your skirt?"

"Nothing. Want to see?"

"It's too early in the day for laughter."

Drunk or not, Niall caught the insult. "Lass, I promise ye what hides under me kilt is anything but funny."

"You're right. Anything that hasn't bathed in decades is probably more likely to send a woman screaming. Or fainting from the smell."

"Why you little harpy." Incredulous, he could only stare at her while she smirked.

"Ah, have we reached the point of pet names? How sweet. I was thinking of dung beetle for you."

He went to lunge at her, prepared to toss her over his knee for the spanking she begged for, but caught the way her body tensed in preparation.

The lass intentionally baited him in an attempt to get him upright. She'd probably tussle with him, do something to unman him like kick him in the balls, and then force him to chase her out into the street where the real troops waited to net him and drag him back to Lucifer. Never!

He'd given the devil his soul. But he'd never promised to loan him his talent. Golf had destroyed his life. He'd rather suffer the taunts of the sweet lass than take up a club again.

Apparently, she came to the same conclusion because she sighed. "I really hoped we wouldn't have to do this the hard way."

"Hard is right. Come sit on my lap, and ye will see just how much." He patted his knee, surprised to note his words held truth. For the first time in a *long* time, his cock roused itself for something other than a piss. What a shame she'd probably not let him use it.

Fascinated by the surge of blood to his groin region, he didn't catch her leaning forward to grasp the table. He did, however, watch with a bit of incredulity, though, as she hefted it and flung it out of the way, sending it crashing into one of the creeping shadows.

Damn. The lass had some strength in those pearly white arms. Still, a little bit of muscle was no match for a full-grown male like himself. He crooked a finger at her and beckoned. "Come over here and wrestle something a bit harder."

"Eager, are we?" she taunted with curved lips.

"Like a virgin in a brothel, lass."

"Such eloquence. No wonder the girls are beating down a path to your door."

"Don't you mean a path to my dick?"

"More like a weed-whacker."

Oh, that comment got a wheezing cough of a laugh. He

would have retorted; however, time was up. Before she could make her next move, or comment, the shadows surged from the corners, hungry for her lively spirit.

Given her attitude and remarks, Niall really didn't feel inspired to come to the obnoxious harpy's aid. Altruism wasn't something Niall usually practiced. His idea of mercy usually consisted of a quick death versus a prolonged screaming one—it all depended on his mood. Given his moral views on helping the weak, he planned to do what he usually did. Sit back and enjoy the action. Yet...he quite enjoyed the lass's fiery nature, even if it was unwomanly.

In his day, women didn't question their lords, or men. They did as they were told. They catered to men. They knew their place. They also wore skirts down to their ankles, hiding their feminine attributes. Sure, times had changed. He'd seen the news and watched as they burned bras—an act he whole-heartedly approved given the infernal things never wanted to come off. They wanted equal rights. He could handle that, but in return, they could fight their own damned battles. Even unfair ones such as the one the woman before him faced.

However, this outspoken lass managed something very few had and in just a couple minutes time. She'd gotten him to forget he hated being alive—or given his vampiric state, was the more correct term undead? Whatever the case, she'd gotten him to feel something other than misery. She made him want to...well, fuck, for one. Didn't that deserve some kind of acknowledgement? And he could use some exercise. He'd not swung his sword—flesh or metal—in quite some time.

Despite how thinking with his cock paid off last time, he nevertheless lunged from his seat, straight at her, determined to practice some rusty chivalry and tuck her behind him out of harm's way. Bad move. He almost got a close shave for his magnanimity. Only quick reflexes, dulled slightly by the alcohol marinating his system, had him ducking the lightning-quick draw of the axe strapped across her back. He lost a few locks of hair despite his quick action, though. The demon behind him? Not as lucky.

It seemed it wasn't Niall's head she targeted, but the miscreant using him as a shield to sneak up from behind. He didn't have time to admire her quick handiwork or express his disbelief about the fact she could even wield the massive weapon with enough strength to decapitate a minor demon. Violence erupted, and as usual, Niall ended up in center of it, but for once, not only did he not instigate it, he didn't fight alone.

Swinging his fists and connecting with pulpy flesh, he jumped into the battle with a berserker cry and glee. Nothing beat a good old-fashioned fight, even a fight where his services weren't required. It didn't take long for him to grasp an interesting fact. The lass required no man's aid. Despite appearing all woman on the outside, she possessed a warrior's spirit and skill. He paused to admire her agility because, hot damn, she was a sight to behold.

Swinging her axe like an extension of her body, the yellow-eyed lassie took on the wraithlike demons who dared attack. Without pause or undue exertion, she twirled her weapon, and wherever she made contact, limbs hewed off and dark fluid erupted in a geyser.

Most women Niall knew cowered or hid from violence. Or at least they did in his time. The gore and wailing deaths of the creatures didn't slow his mouthy lass one bit. On the contrary, a fierce smile stretched her lips, her eyes glowed an excited, maleficent gold, and laughter bubbled from her. Wondrous, joyous laughter, which coincided with each deadly swing.

"Take that, you bastard," she crowed. "Die, you spawn of the pit," she cackled. "Oops, don't lose your head now," she taunted as another dropped to the ground. Her attitude lit something within him, a fire he'd thought to never feel again. It warmed his undead heart—and gave him a major boner.

Fascinated, and aroused, he watched as she danced among her attackers until she stood alone, the other patrons giving her a wide, respectful berth lest she turn her attention to them. Despite her adept handiwork, Niall stood his ground and clapped when she pirouetted to face him once again.

"Fantastic, lass. Beautiful axe work." For a female. On the one hand, Niall had never been so disturbed in his life by a scene of violence with a woman at its apex and, while at the same time, so turned on.

Leaning on the haft of her weapon, only a slight sheen of sweat glistening on her skin—skin he wanted to lick— she gave him a partial bow of acknowledgement. "Now that we've ascertained I can beat your hairy arse in a fight, will you come willingly?"

She thought she could take him? She obviously didn't

know of his reputation. More rusty laughter croaked from him. "Apparently, no one warned you about me. In my time I was known as the Fearsome McGregor."

"Never heard of you."

"Sure you have. I killed hundreds with my sword and bare hands."

"Sorry. Still doesn't ring a bell and I've seen all the Pit documentaries on the greatest marauders currently in residence."

"I was a laird!"

"And I was a queen. Big fucking deal. Now, if you're done trying to convince me of your greatness, we have places to go and a devil to see."

"The answer is still no."

"Um, did you not just watch me in action? Do you really think I care what you think? Willing or not, you are coming with me." She thumped her axe head on the floor for emphasis.

Hot damn if he didn't want to take her on and teach her a lesson. Strangely, though, he also didn't want to hurt her, which was what would happen if she persisted in her foolish attempts to get him to accompany her. But what could he do to avoid a fight? Something he'd not ever done in his previous life.

"Oh, I'll *come*." He winked, a flirtatious act he'd not thought himself capable of. "First, though, you'll have to catch me."

And, with those challenging words, Niall waved goodbye and teleported away.

3

WHERE THE FUCK did he go?

Aella stared at the spot her target had vanished from and cursed. "Fuck. Fuck. Fuck." Whirling on her heel, she fixed the barkeep with a fierce stare. "Where has the Scot gone?"

The massive black demon with one horn and scars all over his body dared to shrug and turn away. Seriously? Had he not just watched her decimate most of his patrons? How dare he ignore her question!

With a low growl, she leapt across the room, landing on the counter, one fist immediately grasping the bartender's remaining horn while her other held a dagger to it. Yanking his head back, she forced him to look at her.

"I asked you a question, demon," she snarled.

He didn't seem to care. "You are asking for trouble, hunter."

"My actions are sanctioned by the dark lord himself."

"You are not currently in the imperial ring. His word holds little sway out here."

"Maybe, but my sharp knife says you will give me the answers I seek." To show intent, she dragged the tip over his skin, and a dark bead of blood welled. She was ready for him when he bucked, intending to throw her balance off. Not the brightest of moves. Aella never uttered empty threats. It took just one slice of her sharp blade to sever his horn. Screaming, he slapped a clawed hand to the gushing hole in his head.

"You bitch!"

"And your executioner if you don't start talking. Or should I take off a few more body parts first for fun?" She smiled sweetly as she aimed a pointed glance down.

He blanched, and his earlier defiance melted. "The Scot's got one of those amulets. Them teleporting ones."

"I figured that. But where did it take him?"

"To his tower."

"You mean he has a home? My sources claimed this bar as his permanent residence."

"Because he rarely leaves here. He does, however, have a place, by the bluffs in the ninth ring, right on the edge of the Darkling Sea." Now that he'd chosen to talk, the barkeep couldn't give her enough details of the Scot's lair. It didn't mean Aella spared his life. As his body slumped to the ground, the eyes staring sightlessly, she stood and addressed the remaining patrons watching in silence. None dared interfere.

"Let this be a lesson to those who would defy our lord. Or more aptly, defy me."

Wiping her dagger clean, she sheathed it and strode

out of the dirty bar into the even filthier street. Fuck, she hated visiting this part of Hell. However, her location wasn't to blame for her mood. The hairy Scot had bested her. How irritating.

Aella prided herself on not getting taken by surprise and of covering her bases. Her attention to detail was what made her a good hunter. Yet, somehow, in her research, which in her defense didn't amount to much, the Scot's file sparse, she'd failed to note the bastard had a secondary residence. Which really sucked because having never seen it before, she'd have to translocate to the nearest portal in the ninth ring and probably walk. Ugh. Just another thing the Scot would end up sorry for when she caught up to him. And, this time, she wouldn't play nice.

4

Niall eyed the waves buffeting the cliff, the dark churning waters slapping against the rocks and scattering droplets in a lighter gray spray. For the most part, the River Styx meandered through the nine rings of Hell, its murky poisonous waters fairly calm except when one of its deadly denizens popped up to say hello to the fresh souls traversing. Charon, the robed entity who navigated the newly damned from the outer shore to Hell itself, apparently had a deal with them. Rumor had it he fed the water monsters and made bargains to have them scare the newbies whilst making himself appear grand, battling them off with the pole he used to guide his boat.

But those creatures in the Styx were like babies compared to the humps he saw undulating here on the outer edge of the nine circles where the Styx spilled into the roiling sea. Where the vast ocean with its wild waves and endless horizon went was anyone's guess. None who sailed its waters ever returned. Niall had almost joined an expedition or two just to find out, yet while he wanted to end his existence, he feared more ending up the meal of a kraken or other large sea monster, undead in its stomach, spending eternity getting digested and resurrected.

Damned cursed bargain.

As he stood upon the cliff, he couldn't help but reflect, as he had hundreds of times before, the events that brought him to this place. A depressing tale of male stupidity that, thankfully, had never made it to song or history, probably because he'd killed the bards who dared put lyric to his shame.

It all began with his lust for a woman. Not just any woman. Fionnaghal McTavish...

CENTURIES BEFORE...

ONLY ONE STROKE AWAY FROM THE WIN. I CAN DO THIS.

Kneeling in the spongy growth, Niall eyeballed the ragged hole and gauged the distance between it and his ball. An easy shot if he didn't choke, and the moment he'd dreamed of when he'd made his bargain with the devil— in blood on parchment longer than his arm, with tight writing and clauses that made his head spin. The one thing he made sure of, though, in all the fancy wording, was that in exchange for his soul, he'd be the world's greatest golfer. But mastering the sport wasn't all he'd get; he'd also get his chance to become more than just laird of his small demesne.

See, Niall had made a wager with his long-time rival,

Donnan. Whoever won this match would earn not just the title of baron, but the hand of the fair maiden Fionnaghal too. Niall's one true love. A fair-skinned, red-haired maiden, she'd captured Niall's heart from the first time he'd glimpsed her—and it didn't hurt she was her father's only bairn, making her heir to some of the richest land in Scotland. Soon to be his land.

The watching crowd held their breath as Niall stood from his crouch and set himself in position. A stiff breeze made his tartan flutter about his bare knees. Time for the devil to keep his part of the bargain. He had so far, ensuring Niall remained a point ahead most of the game until an unfortunate stroke of luck on Donnan's part on the sixteenth hole landed him straight in the cup, tying them for strokes. The bastard.

Niall needed to sink this putt for the win. He pulled back his club and swung, a light tap to send the little ball jouncing across the green. It tumbled and rolled, losing speed fast in the uneven terrain. Niall eyed it intently. Five feet. Four. Three. Two. It teetered on the edge of the hole.

Fuckin' hell.

A murmur rose, and Niall just about cursed aloud when it toppled in. The excited roar of his clan rose in a wave of sound as he claimed victory.

I did it! I won!

Everything for a while after that glorious moment blurred. He remembered in snippets the way his clan bore him up on their shoulders and carted him back to the castle, where the baron clapped him on the back and congratulated him. He remembered smiling at Fionnaghal, who looked away, ducking her head in obvious shyness as was proper for a woman of her station.

With everyone gathered, and in the eyes of his clan and that of his soon-to-be father-in-law, Niall pledged himself to Fionnaghal. The wedding was set for three days hence. With the formalities out of the way, they feasted, celebrating his good fortune. Wine and ale flowed freely, much of it into Niall's mouth.

Hours later, a little drunk—make that a lot—Niall made his way to the castle ramparts, hoping for some fresh air—and a place to piss. The latrines on the main level overflowed, and besides, he took perverse pleasure in pissing off the wall. Soon to be his wall.

Hauling his cock out from under his plaid, he balanced on the parapet and surveyed the land surrounding him. *My land.* And it had only cost him his soul. Bah, like he had any use for the thing.

Some would have named his bargain with the devil as harsh. However, more than just the title and land seduced him into making the choice. The beautiful Fionnaghal with her straight white teeth, her creamy white skin, and long auburn locks played a big part. Niall loved her. Wanted her.

Many a Scot had tried for her hand. Many a man dreamed of getting between her white virginal thighs. Niall beat them all, even the annoying Donnan. So what if she seemed reticent and less than overjoyed? Once she got to know him, she'd come to love and respect him like a proper wife should and, with those wide hips of hers, birth him many strong sons to carry on his name.

Leaping from the stone wall, Niall was on his way to

rejoin the festivities when he heard the moans. A couple had escaped from the revelry and were indulging in some carnal fun. Lucky bastard. In the castle of his betrothed, Niall wouldn't find that kind of indulgence this night. He had too much respect for his bride-to-be, but it didn't mean he didn't envy him. After today's blood-pumping win, he wouldn't have minded a little fucking to celebrate, but he'd have to wait a few more days for his wedding. He couldn't wait to make his sweet Fionnaghal into a true woman. To have her moan his name in pleasure.

"That's it. Take it, my slut." The familiar rumbly voice of his nemesis Donnan carried clearly.

Oh ho. It seemed the loser got lucky. Curious as to which female his rival had chosen to sate his disappointment, Niall crept close to the sounds of flesh smacking.

What he beheld froze him. Donnan pumped much like the animals in the fields, his buttocks exposed and flexing as he plowed between a pair of white thighs and sowed his seed. Sowed his seed on a very willing Fionnaghal, who cried out encouragement to her lover. "Oh, Donnan. More. Give me more. Make me forget that ugly beast Father is making me marry."

Now many a man would have lost his mind at this point. And with good reason. Most would have drawn sword and meted justice in the form of violence and bloodshed for the dishonor done to him. But Niall didn't lose his temper; instead, an icy calm fell over him. He returned to the party and got royally drunk. He stayed drunk for three days until the morn of his nuptials.

Wearing his cleanest plaid, his hair braided, his sword polished and strapped to his back, his knees bare, and his pride sharp, he said the ritual words that bound him to Fionnaghal. He looked into her treacherous face and cursed the bargain he'd made to win the faithless bitch.

Once the deed was done and he found himself married to the slut, he allowed them to be carried to the feast. Of the wine and ale, he abstained. Silently, he brooded, alone in a sea of well-wishers, simmering at the ill done to him. Fionnaghal had the nerve to look guileless, smiling and laughing, the picture of a happy bride. Even blushing as a proper virgin should. But Niall knew better.

As for Donnan, he tossed smug smirks Niall's way. It would have taken a more temperate man to ignore the unspoken taunt. But, first, Niall did his duty.

He took his bride to bed, and when she pretended discomfort during the breaching, he bit his tongue lest he call her out. Niall finished claiming his bride, taking no pleasure in the act. Like killing in battle, it was something he needed to do for victory so that she couldn't claim he'd not completed his role. He was ready for the vial of blood she pulled from beneath her pillow to complete her subterfuge.

He caught her slim wrist and pried the bottle from her hand. "You won't be needing this," he told her in a cold voice.

Eyes wide, she licked her lips nervously. "I can explain."

"No need. I already know. You really should have been more discreet. I saw you and your lover."

"He forced me," she lied.

"We both know that's untrue." Niall rolled from bed and pulled on his plaid before he buckled on his sword.

"Where do you go, husband?" she asked, not even having the maidenly decency to hold a sheet up to her bosom. Nay, she arched like a practiced whore, trying to distract him.

She failed.

"I go to regain my honor."

Ignoring her tears and pleading to remain silent, Niall strode from the bedchamber back to the gala. He did not pause to acknowledge the ribald jests about completing the act so soon. He did not reply to anyone so great his rage burned. Up to Donnan he strode, pulling his sword as he stalked.

The petty laird, to his credit, did not flinch. He drew his own steel and met his in a clash of metal. Back and forth, they dueled, Donnan on the defense as Niall hammered at him.

Screams asking what happened went unanswered, but all soon guessed the cause of his rage when his disheveled bride appeared, shrieking it wasn't her fault, that Donnan had seduced her.

And, in the same breath, she begged him to spare her lover. "Please. Don't kill him. I'll be a good wife. I promise. You've bedded me. You know I'm willing. I'll do anything you want if you spare him."

Instead, he lopped off Donnan's head.

For good measure, he also chopped off that of his faithless bride, her blustering father, and all who took umbrage with his version of justice. Not many, as most sided with him. Scots did so love a good battle. His new clan united with his old, eager for action. As one mighty force, they marched against Donnan's lands and laid them to waste, erasing his name from the annals of history. Then for shits and giggles, they marched some more, leaving a swath of blood and destruction behind them. Why not? Niall was already damned to live in the pit, might as well populate it with shitheads he could torture for eternity.

As for golf and the deal he made to become the greatest player ever? He never touched a club again.

And he'd kept that promise, 'til now.

A SCUFF OF A PEBBLE, A NOISE OUT OF PLACE HERE ON THE edge of the pit, drew him from his memories of the past and had him whirling. Without much surprise, he beheld the lass from the bar. He'd expected she would show up sooner or later. Tenacity often went hand in hand with ruthlessness.

Looking as delectable as ever, she appeared less than happy as she stalked toward him, her red toga swishing about her knees, her upswept hair bouncing with every step. His cock swelled, his body enjoying the view. Odd, because Niall usually preferred his women more demure and chubbier.

"Took you long enough," he taunted.

"I stopped to have my nails done. Like them?" She held up her fingers to show finely-honed digits painted a deep red. They looked great—and would look even better clawing at his back as he fucked her.

"Pretty. Did you get your pussy shaved too while you were at it? I hear hairless cunts are all the craze nowadays."

Those luscious lips pursed as she approached with undulating hips. "Such dirty language. Then again, what can I expect from a filthy Scot? You're just a step above an animal."

"Aye, lass, I guess I am. As a matter of fact, I'm the biggest stallion ye will ever meet. Hung and ready to go anytime ye are."

"I prefer my bedmates to be clean."

"That's easily arranged."

Possessed by something other than misery for once—playfulness rising in equal measure to his lust—he lunged forward. No longer drunk, his speed took her by surprise. He hefted her over his wide shoulder, and before she could say more than, "Mother fucker!" he leapt off the cliff.

Air rushed past his face as they plummeted, and he laughed while she cursed him out. They hit the warm waters of the sea with a mighty splash, her weaponry dragging them both down. To her credit, she didn't panic like some folks would when finding themselves sinking underwater.

Then again, for all he knew, she could breathe underwater. In Hell, the laws of the mortal world were twisted. The impossible wasn't always true.

Niall, however, required oxygen, or at least, he preferred it. Inhaling water always made him uncomfortable and sick for days. Letting his burden go, he kicked away from her and rose to the surface. His head broke the waves, and he took in a breath. When she didn't immediately appear, he took in a deep breath and prepared to plunge back under to find her.

Not necessary as a sleek head bobbed up and a pair of glowing yellow eyes fixed him, not with the baleful glare he expected, but mirth. "How nice of you to finally take a bath for me."

He couldn't help the quirk of his lips. "Ha. Like a simple dunk will rid me of all the dirt." He'd spent decades layering it on.

Holding up an oblong white lump, she grinned, a malicious leer, which sent a shiver through him. "Then it's a good thing I brought soap."

The horror. The travesty. The...wench! No matter how strong his strokes to escape, she kept up with him, darting in like an otter and scrubbing at him. The ocean around them went white as bubbles frothed to the surface. The final straw, though, had her clinging to his back, her muscled thighs holding him tight—damn but she had the grip of a python. He yelled as she hacked at his wet hair, giving him an unwilling trim.

This game was no longer funny. A bath was one thing, but his hair! He'd spent many centuries growing it out. "You evil harpy. Leave my hair alone."

"I told you to come with me nicely." She panted as she held on to his bucking frame. His attempts to pry her off failed. With his feet kicking to keep them afloat, he could do little more than roll in the water.

Wet clumps of hair floated around them. When his feet finally touched sand, he slogged ashore and flopped to the ground. She leapt out of the way before he could squash her. But she wasn't done with her torture. Back she came, this time straddling his chest, not low enough to take care of the problem between his thighs.

With the blade she wielded so close to his neck, he daren't move much. Sure, he doubted she'd lop his head off; however, he worried about accidentally harming her. Even if the wench deserved punishment as she shaved a few centuries' worth of beard from his face, leaving him smooth-skinned such as he hadn't experienced since his wedding day.

For once, he didn't recall that time with depression or an urge to kill Donnan and his wife all over again. Instead, he wondered what the toga-wearing lass thought of what she saw. And what it would take to get her to reseat herself a little bit lower, say on top of his straining cock.

But I might want to get her to drop the knife first lest she chop it instead of fuck it.

5

Aella expected a lot of things when she tackled the Scot with soap, determined to at least force a semblance of cleanliness on him. What she didn't foresee when she decided to give him a much-needed trim was him caving to her ministrations. Even more unexpected was the attractive man who emerged from the shaggy mess.

Before, he'd resembled a disgusting Sasquatch, all matted hair, rancid stench, and, despite his speech, one step above an animal. Now…now she could see what hid beneath, and quite frankly, it stunned her.

Niall would never be described as a truly handsome man. His features were much too rugged and square for that. His nose too large. His brows too thick, his hair too red, and his skin, freckled. But he bore a strong face. A warrior's face, and with the stench gone, his shirt torn away in their tussle, and his plaid gaping, she could clearly admire the physique with a musculature reminiscent of the gladiators she'd ogled in her youth.

One big difference, though, became evident, and she meant big. Straddling his waist, she couldn't miss the pulsing hard-on currently poking against her backside.

"I see a clean body doesn't mean a clean mind." She arched a brow at him.

Opening his eye, his vivid blue iris fixed her as Niall's lips curved into a slow, sensual smile that sent a shiver through her system, one that went on and on, especially once she spotted his sharp fangs. "Lass, if you don't get off me, all your cleansing work will be for naught because I will take it as an invitation to dip my dick and get sweaty."

Her nose wrinkled. "You really need to work on your come-on lines. I realize you're ancient and all, but those kind of remarks went out with the dinosaurs."

"Does this feel old to you?" He clasped her hips and ground against her ass, transitioning her pleasant shiver into a liquid heat that moistened her pussy.

The shock of it almost made her slit his throat. Aella didn't like it when her body didn't behave as expected. And feeling desire for a Scot wasn't on her list of approved bodily actions. Then again, now that he'd cleaned up, he at least showed potential. *Ugh. What is wrong with me? I am not fucking my target.*

"You got an erection. Big fucking deal. Anybody with access to Viagra can get one nowadays."

"You have an answer for everything."

"But of course."

"Then answer me this? If you're so unimpressed, why is your pussy wetting me stomach?"

"I had to pee."

Biting her tongue at the expression on his face, she

rose from his body, giving him a naughty peek at what she didn't wear under her toga. His eyes fairly smoldered as he stared. To his credit—and her disappointment—he didn't try to touch. Probably a good thing. She'd sliced off the hand of the last idiot to try that without permission.

When he didn't rise from the sand, she asked, "Are you coming?"

"I'd like to."

"With me, you idiot."

"Didn't I already say I'd like to?"

Tapping her foot, she glared at him. "Would you stop turning everything I say into a sexual innuendo?"

"No. This is the most fun I've had in a long time."

"Well, I'm glad one of us is enjoying ourselves."

"Lighten up, lass. You only live once."

"Says the drunk I found wallowing in a bar in the most disreputable part of Hell."

"I have my reasons."

"And how old are they?"

He scowled. "None of your business."

"Did I offend you? Good."

"How is making fun of my misery good?"

"I can't abide idiots who mope."

"I wasn't moping."

"Then what do you call what you were doing?"

"Getting drunk."

"For how many centuries?"

"Why do you care?"

"I don't. I just can't stand people who fuck up their mortal life and then end up in Hell blaming everyone but themselves for the mistakes they made."

"I didn't make a mistake. I was wronged."

"And?"

"And it wasn't fair." His lower lip didn't jut, but there was no mistaking the pout.

"Boo-fucking-hoo. I was a queen until I was wronged too. Do you see me acting all depressed? Fuck no. I had a temper tantrum, killed a few things, and got on with my life." Mostly. She'd yet to get involved in a serious relationship since her mishap. But at least she'd not given up, not like a certain vampire Scot.

"I tried killing those who wronged me. It did nothing for me."

"What did happen to you?"

"I sold my soul to the devil so I could be the greatest golfer ever."

"But you don't play golf."

"Because the game I won, the shot that should have given me a rosy future, ruined it."

"So?"

"What do you mean so? Did you not hear me? Golf ruined my life. Because of it, I murdered hundreds."

A low whistle left her. "Nice. Wish I could have done the same."

"Why didn't you?"

"In my case, those who screwed me over were gods. Greek ones. They've got that whole immortal thing going for them."

"You pissed off some Greek gods? How?"

"I'd rather not discuss it. Unlike some people around here, I don't live in the past."

"I'm not living in the past."

47

"Then get off your fat, lazy, skirted ass and come with me."

"But I don't want to."

Funny, he said it, but without his previous fire. Actually, she got the crazy feeling that her Scot wanted out of his depressing rut; he just didn't know how to do that. She decided to extend a helping hand.

He eschewed it, springing to his feet and shaking, droplets spraying.

"Would you stop that? You're worse than a wet dog."

"You were the one who said I need a bath."

"You needed one. I, on the other hand, was perfectly clean and dry."

"Next time you bring some soap, maybe you shouldn't forget the towel."

Plucking at the damp fabric clinging to her curves, she noted how his gaze strayed and fixed on the delineation of her puckered nipples protruding through the cloth. "Got any towels up at that shack of yours?"

"Yes, along with a warm fire."

Good, because here on the outskirts of Hell, the air was noticeably cooler, and the ever-present sifting of ash almost nonexistent. The heat of the furnace, which kept the pit from freezing, barely reached this distant edge, and she shivered.

The Scot led the way, following a barely discernible track up the cliff side, which angled left to right and required a sure foot lest a misstep send the unwary tumbling. Curious at his docile acceptance of both her grooming and presence, she couldn't help but question.

"So, have you had a change of heart? Are you ready to come with me willingly?"

"I don't want to golf. But—" He turned to peer at her over his shoulder. "I will come with ye to see Lucifer and tell him myself."

"Why?"

"Because ye shouldn't have to face his wrath at my refusal."

She snorted. "Lucifer's not going to punish me if you say no. And that wasn't what I was asking. I mean, why won't you golf?"

"I have my reasons."

"Afraid you've lost your touch?"

"There ain't nothing wrong with my touch, lass. I can assure ye of that. Or, better yet, I can show ye." The naughty grin he aimed her way made her stumble, and she might have tested her ability to fly had he not halted abruptly and held her back with a quick hand.

"If you're so confident, then why not give our lord what he wants?"

"First off, there isn't anyone who can make the devil into a half-decent golf player. Have ye seen the bastard play?"

"So you're scared of ending up like his last caddy?"

A disparaging sound escaped him. "His last caddy was an idiot. Any fool knew not to use the four iron on that hole. He deserved what he got."

"If you're not scared, then why not play? I mean, you sold your soul to be the greatest golfer. Why not use that skill?"

"Why do ye fucking care?"

"So long as you come with me, then I don't really care. Once I hand you over to Lucifer, you and he can hash it out. Me, I just want to get home and watch the season finale of *Game of Thrones*." And have a long hot shower followed by a round with BOB to cure her sudden urge for Scottish meat.

It seemed she wasn't the only one who could pry. The Scot, no longer so reticent, prodded her. "How did a lass like ye become a hunter?"

"What do you mean a lass like me?"

"Look at ye." He waved a hand vaguely in her direction. "Ye are much too pretty for one."

"Are you implying because of my looks I'm not good at my job?"

"Ye seem better suited to a different lifestyle."

"If you say pole dancer or whore…" She put a hand on the leather-wrapped grip of her axe.

"Calm down, lass. I said no such thing, although, ye would make a killing in either profession. I just meant, with your obvious feminine attributes, a lass like ye shouldn't have to work."

A giggle slipped past her lips. "Did you just imply I'd make a good trophy wife?"

"Aye. A pampered one, of course," he added with a wink.

"Are you proposing?"

His turn to stumble, but thankfully, they'd reached level ground, so she didn't have to stop his brick house of a body from falling down the cliff. "I'm not husband material."

"Why not? You're a man. You have a castle, of sorts,"

she added as she eyed the stone tower with its patched and thatched roof.

"Did ye not hear? I was married once."

"Let me guess, she was the love of your life, and once she died, you swore to never love again."

"Oh, I swore to never get married again, right after I killed her."

And with that shocking announcement, he strode into his abode, leaving her with her jaw hanging.

6

WHY NIALL DROPPED that bombshell he couldn't have exactly explained. The lass had taken him aback with her jesting about proposing. More shocking, he'd immediately pictured the violent hunter in a gown of plaid—his colors, of course—striding toward him with a wildflower bouquet, a fierce smile on her lips, and the axe strapped across her back. A wild bride for an untamed Scot.

An insane fantasy.

He barely knew the lass. Wanted to fuck her, yes, but marry? Like bloody hell. But he'd meant what he'd said to her. Warrior woman or not, the huntress of many layers deserved a pampered lifestyle, her every wish catered to. It was how he would have treated such a treasure. How he would have treated Fionnaghal if she'd not betrayed him.

Entering his simple keep, his nose tickled at the dust layering the sparse furniture. What a change from the castle he'd lived in when alive. Back then, only the most lavish of items would do. Rich tapestries had covered his stone walls, and gleaming and carved wooden furniture with plump cushions graced every room. He drank from gold goblets, ate from fine porcelain plates, and had broken more than a few when his temper was roused. He'd employed only the best chefs and servants to serve his needs. Money meant nothing to him, so he spent it without care. Why not? He'd no progeny to deed his wealth to. No woman to spoil. In the end, everything he'd fought for, all he'd achieved, everything he'd bought didn't bring him happiness. Didn't give him back the soul he'd bartered. Didn't give him peace. *And it certainly never found me love.*

Once dead, he descended to the pit where he'd expected his mood to change. Wrong. All his emotional baggage came along with him. There was no escape, and he discovered he couldn't abide hanging around other people, even the damned. He'd taken this simple keep from the demon who owned it, wanting to live as far away as he could from everyone. The solitude proved worse; hence why he'd taken up residence, almost permanently, in the bar. Biding his time. Waiting for…what?

An end to his existence?

For the sense of betrayal to fade?

For a certain lass to arrive?

She sneezed behind him. "Ever hear of a Swiffer?"

Flinging open a cupboard, he grabbed at the linen stuffed inside, almost threadbare but dry. "Dusting is woman's work."

"Showing your age again, old man."

He'd show her old. Whirling, he tossed a dry cloth at

her and, as she caught it, undid the fastening to his soaked plaid. With a shrug, he dropped it to the floor.

She ogled him, probably because he gave her something to ogle. Hands on his hips, erection jutting forth—a mighty one he'd not experienced in centuries—he smirked at her. "Does this look old to you?"

"Ack! I'm blind. Old man dick alert. Cover it up." She protested with her mouth, yet her eyes remained locked on his bare body. He swelled to an even mightier size. "Good grief. Just how big does that thing get? Should I duck and cover before it explodes?"

"Do ye never stop talking? I swear, lass. Ye chatter enough to drive a man insane. If I were your husband, I'd gag you." A subtle thrust of his hips let her know with what.

She clamped her lips shut, but interestingly enough, she didn't turn away. Nor did she blush. Brazen wench. Still naked, he strutted past her, feeling more than seeing her turn to watch as he knelt before the cold fireplace and tossed a few dry logs in. A strike of flint and he coaxed a flame to life.

While he'd taunted her into silence, he found he missed the dulcet mockery of her voice. He also wondered what she did behind his back. Did she rub the coarse linen over her delicate-skinned body? Did she stand naked in his home? Her pussy still damp? Her mouth still defiant? Wearing only those decadent snakeskin boots?

If his cock swelled any farther, it would probably explode like she jested. Attempting to act casual, he turned around and almost groaned in regret as he noted the threadbare linen covering her, sarong style. The wet lump of her toga hit him in the chest.

"Hang that by the fire, would you? I didn't bring a spare, and I refuse to escort you back wearing a rag." Head held high, her imperious tone and attitude begged an answer.

"I am not your servant." He flung her robe into the snapping flames at his back then smirked at her screech of rage as her toga sizzled.

"What did you do that for?"

"Because."

"What part of I don't have anything to wear did you not grasp, Scot?"

"My name, lass, is Niall."

"And mine is Aella, not lass. Use it or—"

"Or what?"

"I'll rip your tongue out and feed it to the carrion birds."

"I'd like to see ye try." He dared her. Purposely. She growled, and her eyes narrowed to the merest slits. Her whole body vibrated with irritation.

He'd never been so fucking turned on.

With nothing to lose, he decided to see how far he could go. He treaded toward her on bare feet, entering her personal space, crowding her. She held her ground, glaring, lips tight. He saw her hands tense at her sides, ready to respond to whatever threat he planned.

But he had a different kind of assault in mind. One of his hands darted forward and clasped her by the wet ponytail hanging over her shoulder, and he yanked her to his bare chest before slanting his mouth over hers.

For a moment, she held herself rigid as he let his lips slide over hers. Then, she bit him, hard enough to draw blood. He chuckled softly. "So ye like it rough? Lucky for both of us, so do I."

Before in their interactions, he'd let her think she could best him by tempering his strength. No longer. His free arm wrapped around her waist, hoisting her, and drawing her flush with his body. His mouth went from coaxing to demanding, his fangs, the darned things he'd inherited as one of Satan's bartered souls, descended.

How he hungered. Not just for her blood, which surely tasted decadent, but for her. Her body. Her womanly essence. Her scream of ecstasy.

He showered her with hard, nibbling caresses. She didn't give in easily. She twisted in his grip and gnawed on his lower lip. Her tongue dueled with his, but it was half-hearted, the rapid racing of her heart giving away her excitement. Finally, after her token attempt to escape, with a moan of surrender, she softened in his arms and returned his passion tenfold.

Sweet fucking hell. He'd not expected that. And he'd definitely not expected the inferno that swept him and totally sabotaged his plan to disarm her. Her arms, trapped at her sides within the band of his, still left her hands free to clutch at his hips, her fingers digging into his flesh, her lower body grinding as best as it could against him.

He tugged her hair, tilting her head back, leaving the panting sweetness of her mouth to drag fiery caresses down the column of her neck until he nuzzled the top of her breasts. He realized she muttered, and when he caught the words, he groaned softly.

"Don't stop there. My nipples need some attention. Bite them. Suck them."

Demanding wench, more vocal than he was used to, but he was more than happy to comply. Loosening the vise of his arm around her torso, he gave himself some room to work with. His teeth tugged at the linen. It fell away, baring her glorious tits. He rubbed his face between them, and her hands wiggled free from the trap of their meshed bodies, but not to push him away. Nay, not his lass. She dug her fingers into his scalp and guided his mouth to an erect nipple.

"Suck it," she demanded.

He bit instead, the sharp tips of his fangs digging in. She gave a little yell. He growled and bit her again before taking the tip of her breast into his mouth. Her strong body bucked against him and almost threw them off balance. Releasing her ponytail, he hoisted her until her legs could wrap around his waist, and he walked them to the nearest wall where he pressed her up against it.

Anchored to the stone, her body was his for the taking. With her eyes closed, her cheeks flushed, and her lips swollen from his earlier embrace, Niall proceeded to pleasure the lass, and as a result, himself.

AELLA COULDN'T HAVE SAID HOW IT HAPPENED. ONE moment she'd gone from annoying the Scot—and enjoying it—to begging him to suck her breasts. He did so with great gusto and talent, drawing her aching peaks into his mouth, swirling his tongue over the sensitive skin, nipping at the tips. Each erotic caress served as a jolt to her pussy. Each lick. Each nibble. Every suck only served to rouse her burgeoning desire higher and higher.

Barely realizing it, her hips ground against him, her wet core pulsing against his lower stomach. What a waste when she could feel his erection straining just beneath. Loosening the grip of her legs around his waist, she let out a growl of frustration when she couldn't get his cock positioned where she wanted it. He was too long and their bodies too close.

His mouth left off its decadent torture of her breasts to whisper at her ear. "Need something, lass?"

"Fuck me."

"You want my cock?"

Did she ever! He rubbed the head of it against her clit, and she shuddered, the muscles of her channel spasming.

"Give it to me."

"And if I don't?" he teased, dragging it across her trembling slit.

With her fingers still meshed in his shorn hair, she found it simple to yank his head back and mash her mouth against his. She slid her tongue into his mouth, dancing it along his, merging their breaths, furthering their passion.

With a groan, he gave her what she wanted. In slammed his dick. Fuck yeah. Long, thick, and ready, his cock was up to the challenge. Without hesitation, he sheathed it within her, and she clenched. Oh, how she clenched. The muscles of her pussy clung to him, welcoming his girth, reveling in the way he stretched her. Pulling back, he had to fight the pull of her channel, but the suctioning drag just served to rouse them further. Back he thrust as she sucked on his tongue. They'd gone past words. Past teasing. Their bodies moved in harmony, him plunging, her welcoming. Her desire coiled, wound tighter and tighter, like a python around its prey.

He tore his mouth away, leaving her mewling then moaning as he pressed the tips of his fangs against her neck, pinching the skin. Their bodies still heaved and bucked, a sweaty, rhythmic slap of flesh. In sank his teeth, the pinprick of pain nothing compared to the euphoria that swept her as the enzymes in his saliva entered her bloodstream.

Holy fuck! She might have howled. She definitely made a very unladylike and unsnakelike noise as her climax hit her. With a final squeeze, a deadly choke of her sex, she came in pulsing waves on his cock.

His dick spilled within her, and he moaned his satisfaction into her skin even as he continued to suck at her neck. Throbbing, sweating, their hearts racing in cadence, they rode the climax to its very end.

It was an awesome ride.

Once reality returned, along with her breath and sanity, Aella faced a tiny dilemma. How to extricate herself from the pretzel she found herself in. She started by unwrapping her legs.

He didn't get the hint; on the contrary, with a final lick of her neck, he moved his mouth up and lavished light kisses on her lips.

She turned her head, breaking it off despite her enjoyment of them. He focused his attention on her earlobe, tugging at the sensitive flesh, which, in turn, made her pussy pulse.

She cleared her throat. "Ahem. Mind letting me down?"

"When I'm done."

"I hate to state the obvious, but I thought we were."

"That? That was just an appetizer."

She was about to point out that it took a hard cock to fuck, but it was then she noticed that, while he'd softened a little, he was still quite erect.

Oh my. Well, that was what she got for taunting a man who'd not screwed in decades, if not longer. "We really should get going."

"We will. Once I'm done."

"Well, hurry it up then. I've got places to go. People to see."

"Oh, you'll be going somewhere, lass."

Apparently, nirvana. Despite her attempt at nonchalance, she couldn't stop a gasp when his hand slid between their bodies to find her clit. He stroked it, and a shudder went through her. He rotated his hips, grinding his dick deep, and the just-doused fire of her arousal sparked. Again, he swirled, rubbing against a sweet spot while his finger worked her clit. A gasp escaped her.

With slow, languorous caresses and subtle thrusts, Niall brought her back to the edge.

"That's it, lass. Clench that pussy around my cock," he murmured, his brogue as thick as his desire.

Aella didn't speak, not when she needed the air she heaved into her lungs as her body coiled tighter and tighter. When her second orgasm hit, she did find enough breath to scream.

Then curse because, before the last shudder of pleasure went through her body, he let her go, and her knees, still weak from the ecstasy, folded, dumping her on the floor.

Fucking bastard.

7

PANIC MADE a man do stupid things. A prime example would be dumping the female he'd just brought to climax on her delectable ass with a lame excuse. He did need some fresh air, even if he no longer technically breathed. A hyperventilating vampire would have been hard to explain. When he returned to his abode, after dragging in large lungfuls of sea air, punching a few rocks, and giving himself a pep talk about not letting her get under his skin —or on top of his cock again—she didn't kill him or burst into tears or yell at him for awhile. Nope. Instead, with the regal bearing of a queen, while wearing a worn sheet, she ordered him to, "Get dressed. We've leaving for the inner circle. Now." Under her breath, she muttered, "Asshole."

Okay, so he deserved the unflattering name she called him, and the dirty looks she shot him as they trekked to the nearest portal when he decided to meekly obey rather than fight her any further. She deserved some compensation for his less-than-chivalrous behavior.

In his defense, he'd had to act like an asshole. It was the only way he could quickly separate himself from her after fucking her a second glorious time because he'd no sooner come inside her delectable body than he wanted her again.

Again!

Niall wasn't even sure he liked the lass, and she certainly didn't like him. Yes, she intrigued him. No denying she made his cock hard. But that was no excuse for wanting to cuddle her after sex. Not a good enough reason to want to take her to bed, hike her legs over his shoulders, and make her scream a third time.

And a fourth. Maybe even a fifth.

He didn't understand it. He'd gone centuries without needing to even tug one off. Gone ages without even the slightest twinge in his dick. She sauntered in to his life, and suddenly, he turned into a rutting fucking beast? Worse, a beast who felt things? For her?

Unacceptable. He should chop her head off now for having obviously bewitched him. That had to be it. She'd cast some sort of spell on him. Some kind of love spell or enchantment that made him desire her and want to shower her with attention and worship every inch of her body. Made him want to…

Yeah, with that train of thought running through his head, was it any wonder he didn't indulge in post-coital cuddling but dumped her on her perfect ass? Now if only her unflattering view of him would help him to see her as nothing more than a woman he'd fucked. Instead, all he could do as he stomped along behind her was wonder how she'd look bent over taking his cock. How she'd look splayed on a bed covered in red satin, her hair spread about her, her lips parted and panting.

Time to change his train of thought, and fast before he made some of his fantasies come to life. "So, how did ye become one of Satan's hunters?"

"I fucked the wrong man. Turns out his wife didn't appreciate his straying."

"I wouldn't have taken ye for the type to steal another woman's husband."

"I wasn't. He lied."

"About more than one thing apparently. He was one of those gods you mentioned earlier?"

"One and the same. His wife was a goddess pretty high up the food chain as well. "

He whistled. "You're lucky ye didn't die."

"Greek gods are known for their melodramatic nature. In this case, the goddess thought cursing me would make more of a statement. A permanent reminder to her straying husband, for one."

"It was my understanding another person can't promise your soul to Lucifer."

"No, but a goddess can turn a mortal into a demon with the right spell and sacrifice."

"Fucked the wrong man indeed." Even more curious now, he had to ask. "Which one did ye piss off?"

"Hera."

"As in the Greek goddess hitched to that hairy fellow with the lightning bolts?"

"The one married to Zeus. That would be the one. But

he wasn't hairy at the time, and I didn't know who he was or that he had a wife. The bastard."

"So ye are a demon, not a damned soul? Or a contracted one?"

"Oh, I have a contract with Lucifer. Not for my soul, though. In exchange for my services, I get to use my mortal form."

"You mean you have another side like one of them shape-shifters?"

"I do."

"So what do you turn into? Hellcat? Sexy demoness with a tail and horns? Slavering beast with fangs and warts?"

He grinned at the rude gesture and look she shot his way. "I am glad to see you find my plight entertaining."

"And ye are not answering my question. What are ye when ye are not a sexy, toga-wearing harpy?" He paused walking as it hit him. "Don't tell me you're a harpy for real?"

Whirling in her tracks, she planted her hands on her hips and retorted, "Do I look like a chicken-legged hag?"

"Nay, but you just said your contract with Lucifer let ye keep your human shape."

"Because my demon shape is that of a lamia."

"A what?"

"Lamia? Half woman, half snake."

"Fascinating."

"Not really."

"Does this mean ye are not gonna show me?"

"No."

"Why not?"

"Will you play golf?"

"Nay."

"Then I guess we'll both have to live with the disappointment."

For now. Niall made a mental note to find out more about this so-called lamia demon form. For curiosity's sake, of course.

The nearest portal back to Hell took them a few hours to reach. It wouldn't have been needed if his lass had enough magic to create a translocation door for two. As for his amulet, the magic only went one way, back to his tower. He'd only ever gotten it because the nearest pub to his home wasn't in crawling distance. When a man could sober up before he got halfway to his bed, he needed a better mode of transportation.

He'd still not figured out why he agreed to come. Once he dumped the lass on her naked ass, he could have easily gotten away. With a head start to escape, even the wiliest of hunters would have found it difficult to track him in the wilds of the ninth circle. But he didn't run away.

Instead, he'd pulled out a clean, if dusty, plaid, found her another plaid she could wrap toga style—and which she almost didn't wear for long. The sight of her dressed in his colors made his rambunctious cock swell with lust. Fuck did he want to sink into her glorious sex again.

And he wasn't the only one, apparently.

Walking into the town, more of a tiny village filled with an eclectic mix of inhabitants, he couldn't help but notice the interest she garnered. Make that male interest. He didn't like it one fucking bit.

"Any reason why you're growling, Scot?"

"I'm not growling."

"Yes, you are. And showing some fang. Hungry for a snack?"

Not unless you're on the menu. He thought it, but didn't say it. In lieu of answering her second question, he chose to answer her initial question. "You're drawing a lot of attention."

"Welcome to my world. It's like this everywhere I go. Males find me attractive."

"Conceited, are we?"

"Nope. Just stating a fact. Trust me when I say it's not something I enjoy. Demons and other folk see a pair of tits, and they seem to think they can touch."

"They do, do they?" he rumbled in a low voice.

"Yup. Then I show them the error of their ways. Usually in a permanent fashion. Unfortunately, unlike my friend Katie, my reputation doesn't stop them from trying again."

"Who's Katie?"

"Put it this way, she makes me seem downright gentle. Word of warning, whatever you do, don't go near her."

"Why not?"

"Because her boyfriend is liable to kill you while she cheers him on."

"Sounds like someone I'd like to meet. If she's attractive, I've got no problem helping her become single again. My sword might be rusty, but its edge is still sharp."

Yellow eyes, narrow with fury, glared up at him as Aella stood practically on his toes. "Stay away from Katie."

"Or?"

"Or I'll carve your cock off myself."

"Why, lass, if I didn't know better, I'd say ye sounded jealous."

"Never."

Before she could turn away on that lie, he looped an arm around her waist and drew her up on tiptoe. Lips practically touching, he whispered, "Ye are gorgeous when angry. It's making me horny. Wanna fuck?"

Apparently, she wasn't as turned on as he was.

"Fucking hell," he yelled as she stomped his toes with her damnable—yet still sexy—boots.

Away she spun, ass swinging tartly. "Pig."

Yeah, she insulted him, but was he the only one who noticed how he retained all his limbs? What a woman. Smiling, he stalked after her, leaving a path of body parts behind as he lopped off the limbs of some gawkers. He did have a reputation to maintain for being a miserable, ornery bastard after all.

They located the portal, its guardian changing its mind about charging them a fee when Aella pulled forth her axe, and they arrived in the inner ring, a place Niall hadn't visited since pretty much his arrival. It hadn't changed much. This close to the furnace of Hell, the ash sifted in a constant swirling dust, giving the buildings and locale around them a desertlike feel as the fine grit coated everything and heaped itself in mounds against walls.

Up they marched to the Lord of Sin's castle, the gates swinging open with an ominous creak, intentional, of course. Lucifer did so enjoy the right ambiance. No one stopped them as they made their way in to the keep, the clack of her boots echoing in the vast, soaring hall, the ribbed ceiling arching high overhead.

The secretary, a warted goblinlike creature, waved them through, and Niall entered Lucifer's office on Aella's heels.

"Here's your Scot," she announced, flopping into one of the leather-bound club chairs. The lord of the pit, lining up a putt on his indoor green, didn't even look up. Niall winced as he pulled back—too far—swung, and hit the golf ball much too hard, sending it pinging across the green in a wide arc away from the hole to land amidst a clutter of other white orbs.

Watching Lucifer play was a form of torture worse than many Niall had experimented with over the years.

With a curse, the most feared demon of all bent his putter into a pretzel and tossed it in a corner with the rest of the scrap metal. He had to give credit to the lord of the pit; he didn't give up.

Pivoting to face them, Lucifer deigned to greet them. His lips stretched into a smile, not the most reassuring thing. "You found him!"

"As if there was any doubt." Aella hiked her legs over the arm of the chair and examined her nails. "So does this mean I'm done? My manicurist is expecting me at three."

"Done. For now. But don't go too far. I might have need of your services soon."

It wasn't until the lass made it to the door that Niall realized—with a pang of irritation—he'd rather not see her go. But short of begging her to stay or tackling her—which probably wouldn't go over well—he saw no way of keeping her at his side. *And I don't want her at my side.* On his cock, yes, but that was just his finally awakened libido speaking. He had no interest in the woman herself, and he'd prove it. As soon as his meeting with Lucifer ended, he'd visit a brothel. He just needed to empty his sac a few times, and next thing he knew, she'd end up a distant memory.

"Quite the woman, isn't she?" Lucifer remarked.

"What?" Caught staring, Niall almost stammered. He focused his attention away from the empty door to the Lord of Hell. "More like a pain in my arse. Do ye know the lass gave me a shave and a haircut?"

"Did she charge you for it?"

"No. Of course not."

"Then why complain?"

"Because—ye know what, never mind. Why did ye send her after me?"

"I need you to help me improve my golf game."

"Impossible."

"Listen, Scot, I know you're still miffed about the whole things-not-turning-out-like-you-expected thing, but that was centuries ago. Isn't it time you got over it?"

"I am over it." And it surprised him to realize that maybe he was. But that still didn't change his mind. "However, when I said impossible, I meant more that I can't help you."

"Why not?"

"Because ye suck. Golf is not your sport." Crossing his arms, Niall stated it baldly and waited for Lucifer to strike him dead.

Instead, the Lord of Sin laughed. "Finally, someone who says it aloud. Do you know you're the only one with the balls to admit it?"

"My father always did say I had a large set. If it's any

consolation, I've seen your brother play, and he sucks too."

"Ha. And he thinks he's so fucking almighty."

"The Lord of Limbo, however, and that Zeus fellow, if they've been practicing, they could play a decent game."

That shut Lucifer up. "So you think they'll win the match?"

"Depends."

"On?"

"Whether ye cheat or not like ye did the last time."

A slow smile spread across Lucifer's face. "Would I do something like that?"

"When don't ye cheat?"

"Good point. It's hard maintaining a reputation like mine. But I do my best. However, even though I intend to stack events in my favor, I'd still like to work on my stroke. What do you say we start right now?"

"I am not teaching ye to golf."

"Then caddy for me and give me advice that I can ignore."

"No."

"Why not?"

"I saw what ye did to your last caddy. I am not stupid enough to volunteer for the job."

"No, but you are horny for a certain demoness. What if I let you have her in exchange for your help?" Slyly put and a prospect so intriguing Niall almost opened his mouth to say yes.

He clamped it shut.

"What? No deal? And here I thought you had the hots for her."

"It's lonely out at the edge of the pit." Niall shrugged. "What man wouldn't find her attractive?" And want to fuck her until her glorious sex pulsed around his cock as she clawed at his back and her sweet blood flowed over his tongue. Damn he missed her already.

"She makes you horny." Lucifer stated with a smug smile.

"Doesn't mean I want to have sex with her specifically. A visit to a few whores and I'll be right as rain."

"Then you won't mind if I pair her up with another male? Zeus has requested her as part of his security contingent for the upcoming match. Something about not using his own minions because they're plotting mutiny again. I swear, that has-been god just can't keep his people in check. I keep telling him he needs to kill some of them off, but they're all related inbred idiots. Everyone's a cousin or uncle or something."

Lucifer babbled on, but Niall only heard one word. Zeus. Zeus wanted Aella. Once upon a time, Aella had wanted Zeus. Fucked the bloody god. Just like she'd fucked him. If Lucifer did pair them up, would Aella raise her toga for Zeus? They did have a history. Rage burned in him.

She's mine! No, she wasn't. But tell that to his dick and temper. Even if he had no interest in her, he didn't want some other male touching her, and if he understood Lucifer correctly, he didn't have to let it happen. If he agreed to the unacceptable.

"Let's say I did agree to caddy for ye, what assurance do I have about my safety? Working for ye could be hazardous to my health."

"Kill a few incompetents and everyone fears me." Lucifer grinned. "Fuck, I love being me. Well, I can't blame you for dreading my mighty wrath. If that's all that's worrying you, then consider yourself safe. I promise not to throw you into the abyss like I have my previous caddies."

"Bah. Your last caddy deserved that punishment. We both know I won't make any mistakes. What I'm talking about is when word gets around I've come out of retirement to help ye. I'll be a target. We all know your enemies don't want ye to win."

It never took much to get Lucifer's paranoia humming. Instantly, the devil's eyes narrowed as he darted a gaze around him. He leaned close and lowered his voice. "You're right. Everyone is out to get me. Greatness is such a heavy burden," Satan said with a weary shake of his head. "You bring up a very valid point about my enemies plotting. You'll need protection from those who would seek to take you out to harm my game. We can't have that. I need to win! So to keep you safe, I'll give you a set of guards from my personal force."

"Nah. Too obvious. We should be subtle about it and not let on that ye need me too much or are worried about losing me."

"You're right." Lucifer rubbed his chin. "What do you suggest?"

"One guard. A female one. One people could mistake for my concubine or girlfriend instead of a protective guard."

"Why, Niall, you horny bastard. Is this your way of

getting Aella back? You know you could have just asked." The devil caught on to his plan.

"Aella? Nope. I wasn't even thinking of her," Niall lied. "But, if she's the best ye got kicking around, then I guess she'll do."

Lucifer smirked. As if Niall could lie to the Lord of Sin and not get caught, but the pretense soothed his ego.

"Done. So when do we start my lessons?"

"Tomorrow. Bright and early. I've got some business to attend to first. Send the lass to me in a few hours. I've got some fucking to catch up on first."

"I wish I could join you," Lucifer replied almost mournfully, "but Gaia's got this stupid rule about not seeing other people while we're a couple. I tell you, if she didn't have a pussy tight enough to almost rip my dick off, I wouldn't put up with her weird notions of fidelity."

"I heard that!" a female voice shouted from seemingly nowhere.

A scowl crossed Lucifer's face. "Would you stop spying on me, woman?" he bellowed back. Laughter was his reply. A corner of his lip curled in amusement. "Darned female. She does on purpose to stalk me. She knows how it turns me on."

"Lucky for me, I don't have to worry about pissing anyone off with me fucking habits," Niall taunted. It wasn't as if he and Aella were exclusive or in love or something. "I'm off. I'll see ye on the green, or whatever ye use around here as a golf course, seven a.m. sharp."

"Excellent. I look forward to it." Lucifer beamed as he shook Niall's hand, almost crushing his fingers.

Niall left Lucifer's office bemused. *What just happened?*

Exactly how had he ended up not only agreeing to help Satan do the impossible, but saddled with the lass he'd wanted to get rid of?

Because of Zeus, that's why. No way was that fucking Greek god getting near her. Once again, his anger surged, and he paused to examine its source.

Jealousy. Impossible as it seemed, while Niall didn't want the lass, the green-eyed monster within him wanted her with someone else even less.

Not good. He hightailed it to the nearest brothel. Time to prove she didn't mean a thing, and to show the ladies what this Scot hid under his kilt.

8

Aella lolled in the massaging chair as the petite demon with wickedly long, razor-sharp red claws rounded her nails and trimmed her cuticles. Mission complete, she should have been happy she could enjoy a little R&R, but instead she found herself wondering how Niall's meeting with Lucifer went. Did he agree to help? Had her boss killed him? Strung him up by his heels?

Not that she cared. Any punishment Niall suffered was his problem. She didn't give a damn. Yes, she'd fucked the Scot, but only because she was horny and he proved handy. Nothing more. Any male with a big prick would have worked.

Niall was particularly well endowed, though, a reminder her pussy quite enjoyed judging by the quiver that shot through it. Well, she wouldn't be riding that particular dick again. Actually, she didn't plan on ever seeing the annoying man again.

Now if only another irritating male would leave her alone.

"Aella, just the demon I was looking for," Lucifer announced with a wide smile she didn't trust.

"What do you want now, boss?"

"Why, Aella, you don't seem happy to see me. I'm wounded." He clutched his breast where his heart would reside if he possessed one.

"If you were wounded, you'd be unable to talk." Because the first thing she'd carve out would be his tongue.

"So bloodthirsty. No wonder I like you, and it seems I'm not the only one. Your services have been requested."

"By who?"

"By an old lover," he answered with a leer and a waggle of his brows.

"The Scot?"

"What? You fucked my new caddy? I'm shocked. Just shocked," Lucifer exclaimed.

"And I'm confused. You said a lover requested me."

"I meant Zeus, you naughty snake. It seems your old flame wants you to protect him."

"Never. I'd rather stand by and clap as he's taken out. Preferably in a painful manner."

"Glad to hear it because I already promised your services to another, and by the sounds of it, you're already better acquainted than expected. Starting tomorrow morning, you'll be protecting my new caddy by posing as his girlfriend."

It didn't take a genius to figure out whom he spoke about. "Like fucking hell."

"Ah, I do so love it when a beautiful woman curses." Lucifer sighed blissfully.

"This isn't funny, boss. I don't want to protect that rude, ornery Scot."

"Why ever not? It's not as if you don't find him appealing. You did, after all, screw him, more than once too according to my sin-o-meter."

"I made a mistake. It won't happen again." Especially if she stayed away from the kilt-wearing bastard.

"I don't care if you fuck him again or not, so long as you do your job, huntress. I am giving you a direct order. Protect my caddy. I need him to help me win this match, and you don't want to see me upset."

Noting Lucifer's eyes blazed with the fires of Hell and smoke curled from his ears, Aella judged it more prudent at this point to hold her tongue. For now. She might not be able to take her ire out on the lord of the pit, but she knew a certain Scot she intended to tear a strip from.

"Of course, boss. Anything you say. But why wait until the morning to protect your investment? For all we know, your enemies plot now to take him out and weaken your game."

"They have spies everywhere, you know," Lucifer confided, peering around with suspicious eyes.

"Tell me where he's at, and I'll get right on it." She might even spare his enemies the trouble and kill him herself.

"That's my girl. Always eager to do my bidding. If only my own children were as well behaved as you."

She couldn't help screwing with him. "Shouldn't you

be proud that they don't listen, though? I mean, isn't disrespecting your parents one of the original sins?"

Lucifer scowled. "Impertinent snake."

She smiled serenely.

"Don't you give me that grin. I get that look often enough from Gaia when she thinks she's bested me. Which she hasn't. Ever. I wear the pants in our relationship." He puffed out his chest and hitched his trousers. Aella could have sworn she heard feminine laughter.

"Sorry, boss. It won't happen again." *Today.* "So where is our skirt-wearing Scot? Getting sloshed in a nearby bar?"

"Actually, he's getting his knob polished at my favorite brothel." A crack of thunder rumbled the establishment. "Formerly favorite," he yelled at the ceiling.

About-to-get-burned-to-the-ground brothel was Aella's first irritated thought after the announcement. Before she could ask which establishment the Scot doomed with his presence, the Lord of Sin disappeared in a puff of smoke.

Dammit. Nails only half done, Aella hopped out of her chair. She didn't rush because of the news her Scot hadn't even waited an hour to find something he could screw. Of course not. Why would she care? *I don't. He can fuck—grrrr---whomever he likes.* However, her boss had given her a job, and she intended to do it to the best of her ability.

And to do that, she needed to find the two-timing bastard.

It wasn't hard to track down Niall. A giant red-haired Scot in a kilt wasn't something seen often in the inner ring of Hell, and given his less than discreet destination, he was much too easy to follow. With each step she took toward the bordello, her ire increased.

How dare he demand her services as a bodyguard? As if he could just order her up like a menu item. And Lucifer had agreed, the troublemaking prick. So what if the job promised to be an easy one? Aella had better things to do than to babysit one old-fashioned Scot—who'd made her body sing then dumped her on the cold floor. Who even now looked to dip his scurvy cock into another pussy. The bastard.

When she was finished with him, he'd have to piss like a girl.

The madam of the bordello, an Indian goddess with numerous arms and even more tits, tried to stop her at the door. "You can't come in here. This establishment is for male patrons only."

"Get out of my way. I'm here for the Scot."

"He is currently occupied."

One of the madam's many hands latched onto her wrist. Aella arched a brow in disbelief. "You are not seriously thinking of stopping me, are you? I am here on our lord's business."

"I don't give a flying fig. This is my business, and I am saying you stay outside."

Aella didn't give her a second warning. Free hand moving, quick as an adder striking, she grabbed her axe and lobbed the offending limb off.

Black ichor sprayed from the amputated area. "You cunt!"

"I guess I should have warned you that I don't like to be touched."

"Guards!" screamed the bleeding whorehouse owner.

"Oh. If you're looking for the two meatheads guarding the entrance, they kind of lost their heads." Aella shrugged in fake apology, the smile on her lips at odds with the cold glare she bestowed upon the madam. "If you look, though, I think you'll find them in the street. I'm pretty sure one of them rolled under your front step."

More than a few heads rolled as some more demons dressed in uniforms to match the décor came pouring out of woodwork. Aella cursed and swore as she hacked at them.

"Would you get the fuck out of my way?" she grumbled. "I'm trying to do my job." Males! They just never listened. By the time they'd gotten the point she wouldn't be deterred from her destination, she was covered in a layer of bodily fluids, blood mostly, and a few spatters of brain. Not much, though. These types of lowly servants weren't hired for their mental capacity.

All the delays, though, placed her in a really foul mood. She'd wasted too much time. Niall was probably buried balls deep by now, making some slut scream. A fake scream probably, but still, it didn't sit well with her. He wasn't supposed to get any pleasure. How that made any rational sense she couldn't have explained, but blood lust controlling her actions, the thought wouldn't stop repeating itself. Even odder, a little voice in her head kept repeating, *He's mine. Only mine. All mine. Don't touch.* She really needed a vacation if she was taking her job that seriously.

Off she stomped, up the stairs, only to find herself confronted by a long hallway lined with closed doors, each covered in patterned red leather and dimpled with metal rivets. Sound-proofed and solid. Behind which one did her Scot hide?

She refused to abase herself and sniff like some bloody dog. Instead, she resorted to old-fashioned methods. She booted open the doors, one by one, startling the occupants.

Door number one, wrong man. Those white buttocks currently getting whipped by a pair of twin blondes didn't belong to Niall.

Door number two, the flabby gent dressed in garters, stockings, and heavy makeup wasn't her Scot.

Doors number three and four held more wrongness, but interesting apparatuses. She wouldn't mind checking out the swing hanging from the ceiling at a later date.

On she went, getting more annoyed with each portal she opened that didn't reveal the male she looked for.

Then she got to the last portal. She gripped her axe, her palms suddenly sweaty, her anger wound tight, her heart strangely aching. She didn't want to open it and see Niall fucking a woman, but she did want to kill him for fucking another woman.

Damn there were days being a woman confused the hell out of her.

Bringing her foot back, she swung, and the door slammed open, startling the naked female lying on the bed, but not the man pacing in front of it. A naked man with a limp cock, whose hands gestured as he ranted. "The damned lass isn't even my type. She's mean. And cusses. She fights like a man."

"You better not be talking about me," Aella growled,

not throwing her axe at his back like she initially intended. How could she when he'd obviously not partaken in the flesh so freely offered?

Niall turned to face her, the flagon of alcohol in his hand sloshing. His eyes narrowed as he thrust a finger in accusation. "There she is! The source of my problem. Ye are the reason my cock won't work. Ye cursed it."

"What do you mean I've cursed it?"

"It was working fine this morning. Ye can vouch for that. But, as soon as ye went away, I couldn't get the damn thing to rise. Look at it. Limper than a fucking wet noodle."

She did look at it. Recalled how it filled her and brought her such pleasure. Remembered how he'd brought her not once but twice to ecstasy. Under her lustful gaze, it swelled. And swelled. It thickened until it jutted straight from his body.

"Aha. And she proves my point," Niall shouted. "Why will my cock only work for ye?"

"How the fuck should I know?" Aella smirked.

"Because it's your fault."

"I fail to see how it's my fault that you're old and your willy doesn't always work the way it should. Maybe you should look into getting some help."

"I dinna need any help."

"Says the guy bitching about his limp dick."

"It's not so limp now." He propped his hands on his hips and waggled.

Despite the absurd situation, and her irritation, she couldn't help but snort in mirth.

"Dinna laugh at me."

"I'll laugh if I want to." She did just to prove she could, then truly guffawed when his face turned several shades of annoyance and a growl bubbled forth from him.

"You are the most aggravating female ever!"

"Mind telling my boss? It's those kinds of compliments that will boost my statistics when it comes to the employee of the month award."

"I'd rather put you over my knee and paddle your arse."

"I'd like to see you try."

The paid-by-the-hour worker took that moment to interrupt. "Threesomes are extra."

As if reminded of his location, Niall peeked down at his bobbing dick then Aella. "Hold on a second whilst I take care of business, lass." To her shock, Niall turned his back to her and staggered to the bed and the naked whore. He wouldn't dare! *If he lays a finger on her in front of me, it will be the last thing he ever does.* Smacking of jealousy or not, Aella knew her limits wouldn't allow her to watch him fuck another female. Before Aella could stab him in the back, he growled, "Get out."

"With pleasure," she snapped, the twinge in her chest area probably more to do with indigestion from lunch than hurt that he would dismiss her.

"Not ye, lass. Her." He pointed at the whore. "And tell your boss I need the room for the night." Miffed, the prostitute stalked out of the room and slammed the door shut, leaving them alone.

Elation he wanted her to stay eased the pain, but birthed questions she'd rather not deal with. Such as what did he intend? "You know there are hotels that will charge you less for the use of a bed."

"But do they have me, a hard cock, and ye naked?"

"I'm not naked," she pointed out.

"No, you're not. Let me fix that for ye." Aella darted away from his lunge, his fingers just missing her toga.

A growl more animal than man, smacking of definite frustration, left him. "Stand still, would ye, while I strip ye?"

"No."

"So ye wanna fuck with the robe on? Kinky. I like that."

"No." *Yes.* "We are not fucking."

Up went one of his brows. "Why not?"

"Because I am not in the mood." She'd win sinner of the month for sure if she kept up the lies.

"I bet I could change your mind."

"Someone thinks highly of his ancient skills."

"Ye liked my technique well enough this morning."

She certainly had. "That was then. This is now."

"Now is a good time."

"For you maybe, but not for me."

"Why not?" Ever see a muscled, naked man with a massive erection pouting? It was sexier than it should have been.

She didn't give in to temptation. "Because I don't want you." Too late she recognized the extended challenge.

"Yet. Come here and I'll prove you're a liar."

He probably could. Already her damnable body warmed, honey dewed her pussy, and her nipples hardened.

"I didn't come here to fuck you. Lucifer says I need to protect your hairy ass."

"I thought we'd ascertained my arse was perfect this morning."

It certainly was, but that was beside the point. "Would you stop twisting my words?"

"I'd rather twist my tongue around your clit and make ye scream, but ye won't stand still."

Oh fuck, she couldn't help the quiver in her pussy at his words. "I hate you."

"Feeling's mutual, lass, but that don't mean I don't want to fuck ye."

And by all that was sinful, so did she. Worse, she had orders to. According to Lucifer, she was supposed to play the part of his girlfriend. "Just because you've got experience and size doesn't mean I like you or that you own me."

"What's like got to do with it? I'm horny. You're horny. We might as well take advantage of it and this here bed."

When put like that... It did seem practical, and she did admire efficiency. "If we do screw, it's just so anyone spying on you and planning to take you out believes we're a couple." Weak as excuses went, but still it gave her a plausible reason as to why they should.

"Smart and sexy. Excellent plan. What better way to fool Lucifer's enemies than for you to play the part of my girlfriend."

"Except for the fact I kind of left a swath of bodies on my way to find you." Oops. She really needed to get this whole jealousy thing under control. "I guess I might have blown that cover already."

"Or not," he countered. "Actually, this will probably work in our favor. We fought. I visited a brothel to get back at ye. Ye invaded in a jealous pique. We made up and fucked like wild animals."

Ooh, she couldn't help the shudder. His crude way with words did paint such a vivid picture, one she couldn't help but crave. "Plausible. But—" She wagged a finger at him. "I'm only doing this to retain our cover to the outside world." She took a step toward him.

"Of course. We don't like each other. Anything more would be ludicrous."

"Insane."

"Fucked up."

"Totally."

Despite that, they came together in a clash of lips and teeth, their passion instant and fierce, their hunger mighty, even given their coupling less than a day ago. His hands made quick work of her toga, tearing at the clasp and letting it fall to the floor. He didn't seem to mind she wore the stains of battle. On the contrary, the covering of blood and the metallic tang permeating the air along with that of her arousal only seemed to enflame him further. He licked her clean, his vampiric nature coming in handy, and while some might have found themselves turned off by his behavior, as a creature of violence, Aella didn't mind, not when it meant they could indulge in their passion without pause for petty things like a shower.

He fell backward onto the soft mattress, his body the cushion for her fall, placing them skin to skin. She didn't enjoy her position atop him for long because he rolled her under him while continuing to pamper her with kisses and moist licks. It seemed natural to part her legs so he could settle himself between them, just like her hands automatically dug into his scalp as she pressed her lips firmly to his, an unbreakable seal that allowed her tongue entry to dance wetly with his.

Nestled between her thighs, he pulsed, the thick length of his cock trapped but making its presence known. She moaned, wiggling her hips in invitation.

A rumbling chuckle vibrated against her lips. "Impatient, lass?"

"Try horny," she said, panting, not ashamed to admit it, not when the honey pooling at the mouth of her sex gave it away.

"And I'm hungry." With a final peck on her lips, he moved away, only to nibble his way down her neck. Yet, despite his claim of hunger, he didn't pause at the vein that throbbed so rapidly. His interest lay lower. An erect nipple proved his destination, and he latched on to it with a roughness that had her crying in unabashed delight.

Her whole body quivered as he lavished attention on her needy nubs, the tips so tight they ached as he tortured first one then the other. He shifted his weight as he toyed with her breasts, giving him room to insert a hand between her bodies, his fingers on a quest for the moistness between her legs.

"Damn it all, lass. I want to taste ye."

"And you're waiting because…" she teased him, her soft, flirty tone so unlike her. But, as before, everything with Niall was different. He made her feel things. Want things. An intimacy existed between them that somehow had her acting contrary to her usual self. She didn't understand it, but she did know she enjoyed it, although not as much as she enjoyed his mouth when it took her up on her taunt.

Holy fuck. The Scot knew how to make her body sing. Lashing her clit with his tongue, he drank of her honey, his hands holding her still even as she attempted to buck, the sensations too intense.

As if the pleasure of his tongue weren't enough, he inserted a finger. Two. Rough with calluses from sword fighting, his digits provided the friction and penetration she need. They also proved her undoing. Her orgasm hit fast and hard, her channel clenching around his fingers, her body pulsing in time to his thrusts and sucks.

And he didn't stop. Despite her climax, he continued to suck at her moist flesh, to plunge his fingers deep until he found the spot he searched for. Her back arched as he applied pressure on her sweet spot.

"Oh. Fuck. Me," she moaned.

"With pleasure," he growled, finally halting his oral torture. He slid up her body until the thick head of his cock nudged the entrance to her pussy. He thrust into her, stretched her with his girth, and gave her still spasming muscles something to cling to.

She clawed at his back and bit his shoulder, drawing blood in her excitement.

He didn't seem to mind. On the contrary, he took it as an invitation, his head dipping to the hollow where her neck and shoulder met. His fangs sank with exquisite pain and pleasure into her skin until he drew with long pulls at her essence. And, all the while, he moved slowly inside her, ramming and retreating his hard length, creating a rhythm that built both their pleasure.

But their passion couldn't be reined for long. The thrusts became faster, and his swallowing took on a tugging pressure she felt to the tips of her toes. She wrapped her legs around his hips, locking her heels behind his back.

"Fuck me. Harder," she demanded. She begged and she came, came while staring into his vivid blue eyes as he stopped feeding to watch her. In his arms, she shattered as she saw the emotion flickering on his face. She felt something in her burst, and a warmth spread through her at the need she saw reflected on his face, a need she understood and craved. She let go and allowed herself to spiral out of control, knowing she was safe. Trusting him in that moment.

Feeling alive.

9

INTENSE DIDN'T EVEN COME close to defining the moment. Between one breath and the next, it seemed as if the walls and chains he'd bound his heart and emotions in disintegrated. Exploded into tiny pieces and vanished, leaving in its place a warm and protective feeling, one he wanted to lock up and cherish forever. A feeling caused entirely by her. And only her.

He feared he knew what it meant, dreaded it as a matter of fact, yet he didn't run this time or dump her on her ass as he had before. He couldn't. Make that wouldn't, not when it felt so good. So right. *So fucking nice.*

He wanted to bask in the sensation for a bit, so, of course, she just had to open her mouth and ruin it.

"You're squashing me, you giant oaf."

Indeed he was. He quite enjoyed it as a matter of fact. Her? Not as much. She elbowed him until he rolled aside, not far though. He lay on his back alongside her, one arm draped under his head as a pillow, his body still in contact with hers. She didn't move away.

"We should fight more often," he remarked as he stared at the ceiling in the room, the painted murals a disturbing blend of erotic art and impossible sexual situations.

"Fake fight." She just had to argue.

Two could play that game. "Oh, I don't know about the fake part. You seemed mighty pissed when you slammed into here."

"I didn't slam; I kicked."

"Ooh. Big difference. Either way, ye looked like ye'd swallowed a prickly pear sideways."

"Because I was looking forward to a quiet night, but instead, Lucifer gave me orders to guard his new caddy. What happened to 'I'm never golfing again'?" she mocked.

"I'm not. I agreed to give him some lessons and to carry his bag."

"Ooh. Big difference," she sassed in a repeat of his words.

Rolling onto his side, he propped his head on his hand. "I hear disparagement in your tone."

"Give the Scot some underwear as a prize."

"As if I'd wear any. My manparts need to breath."

She snorted. "That is the most ridiculous thing I've ever heard."

"Says the lass who wears nothing under her toga. Let me ask you, since you seem to have a problem with my commando status, why don't you wear any under garments?"

A mischievous grin transformed her from bloodthirsty lass into the girl she once was. He could see why even the gods wanted her. "I don't wear them because when outnumbered, I find a high kick and a flash of certain pink parts gives me the distraction I need to regain the upper hand."

Damn. He suddenly had an urge to spar with her. Then fuck her. Why did everything about her tempt him? "That's evil."

"I know which is why Lucifer pays me the big bucks."

"You enjoy working for the devil?"

"I do. Sure, he's got a messed up sense of humor, and a temper when he doesn't get his way, but he's also fair."

"Let's hope I get to see that side of him when he shows up for practice."

"Don't fuck up and you'll be fine."

"I'm not worried about my golfing abilities."

"That seems cocky given you haven't played in ages."

He shrugged. "I made a deal to be the best. It's like swinging a sword, you never forget how to play." Sometimes he even dreamed of the days when he used to play for fun.

As if she read his mind, she said, "Why can't you admit you miss the sport?"

"Because I don't."

"Please don't insult me. If you didn't, you would have never agreed to help the boss."

"Um, ye do realize he is the Lord of Hell, right? Saying no was never an actual option, no matter what my thoughts were on the matter."

"You caved."

"I negotiated."

"Really? For what?"

He almost said "you." But, given her axe was still in the room and he suddenly found himself with a renewed interest in keeping his head, he wisely didn't say it aloud. "What I find of more interest is your fit of jealousy."

"I was not jealous."

"Oh really?" His lips curved into a mischievous smile. "So ye wouldn't have minded at all if ye'd walked in to find me fucking that female?"

He didn't miss the tensing of her body or the narrowing of her eyes. It stirred him in more ways than one.

"Not at all. You can screw whomever you like. Although…" Her lips curved into their own taunting smile "From the looks of it, your cock didn't like what it saw."

No. It hadn't, damn her. He'd wanted to fuck the whore. Or told himself he did. Yet despite her attractive shape, chosen because she reminded him of a certain lass, she'd stirred nothing in him. It seemed when it came to getting his cock to work, only one toga-wearing demon would do. "What can I say? My dick seems to have taken a liking to ye. It means nothing."

"It better not. I have no intention of becoming your girlfriend for real."

"Good, because I wasn't asking."

"Good."

"Fine."

"Whatever."

They glared at each other. Then dove on each other. They coupled like wild beasts. Fucked as if they'd never fucked before. And when he came, buried in her pulsing sex? For a moment, he could have sworn he touched heaven.

10

WAKING up with a heavy arm over her waist was a new experience, one Aella didn't completely hate. Waking up to see Lucifer leering at her, wearing the stupidest looking hat with a huge pompom, though...

"What the fuck are you doing here?" she screeched.

She no sooner asked than she found herself smothered by a big body as Niall growled, "Ye better have a good reason for barging in."

"I'm half owner of this establishment."

"And?"

"I can come and go as I please."

"It doesn't please me at all."

"Too bad. So sad."

Aella could hear the mockery, and it seemed her Scot did too.

"It's too early in the morn for this," Niall muttered.

"Early? Bah. It's seven a.m. somewhere in the world. So get up, you lazy Scot."

"Cover your eyes."

"Why? Is your junk that small? Afraid I'll laugh?"

Not likely. Aella could vouch for the size and skill of Niall's cock.

Apparently, her Scot knew it too. "Bah. We both know ye envy the size of me dick. I want ye to look away while Aella gets some clothes on."

"Why? It's not like I haven't seen thousands of tits and pussies."

"Aye. But this one's mine."

It was? Aella couldn't help the shiver that went through her at his possessive words. Then annoyance set in. Still squashed and hidden by his bulk, she tensed as she said, "Excuse me, but you don't own me."

"I do until the tournament is done."

"As a bodyguard," she reminded him.

"So guard my body." Niall grabbed at her and slung her in his lap, somehow tucking a sheet around her as he did.

"What are you doing?"

"Using ye as a shield."

Lucifer snickered. "Scot, I am really starting to like your sense of humor."

"Then you would be the only one," she muttered. She pushed at the chest and arms bracketing her. Stronger than a normal woman or not, and a demon to boot, Aella still couldn't get Niall to budge. Simmering, she sulked as they conversed over her head.

"I'm ready for my lesson," Lucifer announced, his tone practically giddy.

"Not in that fucking hat you're not."

"What's wrong with my hat? I bought it at the pro shop."

"Ye look like a bloody idiot."

"Says the man who wears a kilt," Lucifer growled.

"Don't knock it just because ye don't have the knees to carry it off," Niall boasted. "Get rid of the hat. Grab your clubs and meet me at the golf course in an hour."

"An hour? Why so long?"

"Because I haven't showered or eaten. While you're waiting, practice your swing. Actually, don't. Your swing is bad enough as-is. On second thought, just do some exercises to limber up."

"You're right. I am a little tense this morning. See you in an hour. Gaia," Lucifer bellowed as he exited the room. "I need you to stretch my muscles."

"I meant your arm ones," Niall yelled after him.

"According to my girlfriend, it's as big as an arm."

The door slammed shut, and Aella pounded at his chest.

"A shield? That's what I am to you?"

"Why the hysterics? I thought ye would be happy I acknowledged your job."

"Acknowledging me as a warrior whose task is to protect you means letting me up so I can hack at things with my axe."

"But that would have made ye dirty."

"And?"

"I'm hungry."

"I'm not getting it."

"Give me just a moment and you will."

Tipping her onto her back, he somehow ended up

between her thighs, her heels digging into his spine, his tongue lashing her clit. Turned out his idea of breakfast and hers weren't quite the same. She liked his version better. Much, much better.

LATER AT LUCIFER'S PRIVATE GOLF COURSE...

FUCK ME TO HELL AND BACK. NIALL HAD A PROBLEM AND IT was bigger than the one Lucifer posed whenever he tried to hit the golf ball in a straight line.

His plan to fuck another woman and prove once and for all Aella meant nothing had backfired. In a major way. It seemed his cock no longer belonged to him. Nope. It obeyed one female alone. A hottie in a toga who let him pleasure her, but refused him anything else.

When she'd shown up, wild-eyed, bloody, and her expression one of rage, he'd just about expired on the spot. Not because of fear or annoyance at her interruption. Nope. He'd recognized the jealousy and had gotten aroused by her blood-lusting rage. In that moment, when she'd barged in ready to commit murder—*murder for me!* —he'd wanted her so fucking bad. Wanted *her*, not just her pussy or her mouth on his dick, her as a person, her as his lover, her as in his alone. That he felt that way just about killed him when he should have wanted to kill her.

Women were conniving, untrustworthy temptations for men. Or at least the ones he'd known were. And his time in Hell hadn't change that perception, merely reinforced it. Then again, he'd not exactly consorted with the right type. Females-for-hire in bars and brothels didn't exactly make for the best examples.

He vaguely recalled his mother being a sweet, loving, and best of all, loyal type, but then again, he was a little boy who loved and lost his mother at a young age. He knew his father never recovered from her loss and often lamented the fact no other woman could measure up. Niall tended to agree, or had until recently.

Something about Aella made him feel things, strong emotions of a type he'd not experienced before, not even for Fionnaghal. These tumultuous emotions made him want to hit anyone who looked at her. Made him want to build her a castle and surround it with a moat, filled with some of the sea creatures he'd spotted in the Darkling Sea, anything to keep her safe. He longed to see another smile. Hear maybe a giggle of laughter, one inspired by him. Then there was his irrational desire for her, which made him want to rip the clothes from her sexy body and fuck her until she raked him with her nails while he sank his teeth into the delectable long neck she teased him with. Just the thought had him—

"Hey, would you look at that? The ball almost stayed on the green," Lucifer crowed.

Hello, bucket of cold water. Bringing his attention back to the torture before him, Niall held in yet another sigh. Nothing to dampen the ardor like a devil, in eye-popping plaid, massacring a perfectly innocent game. "Ye have to temper your strength. Golf is a lot like fucking. Hit the target too hard and your woman won't want to come back. But tap that sweet spot just right..." He peeked sideways at Aella, who pretended not to look his way but couldn't hide the hard points of her nipples projecting through her silken robe.

"Soft? You want me to be soft?" Lucifer's snort of disgust spoke eloquently. "I've made a career of being hard, in and out of the bedroom. It goes against the grain to show anything mercy, even a little ball."

"Well, if ye wanna fucking win, ye had better learn," Niall snapped back. "Ye have got only two more days before the match. So either smarten up or I'm going to—"

"What, Scot?"

Hmm, perhaps threatening one of the most powerful known beings in the universe wasn't the brightest of courses. Then again, he'd not gotten hired because of his brains. "I'll let ye lose to your brother."

"Lose to that lackwitted goody two-shoes? Never!" Lucifer clamped his lips, hunched himself over his club, pulled back, and gave the ball a light tap. For once, the darned thing stayed on the green. A victory.

"Ha. What do you know? It worked," Lucifer crowed.

"Of course it did."

"Someone sounds testy."

"Probably 'cause we've been at this for hours. I'm taking a break."

"But I was just getting the hang of things."

"So keep practicing. I'm out of here. I need a drink. I'll see ye tomorrow."

"Bright and early," Lucifer yodeled as Niall spun on his heel and left. He couldn't resist a hand gesture in reply, which the lord of the pit chuckled at. Satan possessed the oddest sense of humor. But damn if Niall didn't kind of enjoy it.

Aella kept stride with him as he stalked off, silent for once. A pity, he rather enjoyed her acerbic remarks. But it was probably a good thing because whenever she talked, he was possessed of an insane need to push her up against the nearest wall and fuck her until those perfect lips rounded into Os of pleasure.

"There's no way he can win," she muttered in a low tone once they'd gone a fair distance. "He really sucks."

"Aye, he does. But he's a great cheater."

"And you're okay with that?"

"He's Satan. He can do whatever he damned well pleases. Besides, it's expected of him."

"So much for honor among athletes."

A snort blew past his lips. "Honor? Lass, ye obviously know nothing about sports and men. It's all about winning, at all cost. I would know. I sold my soul to win."

"And yet, from what I heard, you were good enough to do it on your own."

"Perhaps, but my pride required I make sure."

"High price to avoid some embarrassment."

He shrugged. "At the time, I would have done more."

"Was she that good of a lay?"

"I am not discussing my past."

"Chicken."

"Cluck. Cluck." Actually, it wasn't that he feared telling her about his less-than-stellar experience with Fionnaghal and more about not telling his current lover about his ex-wife. Even he knew that wasn't done.

Lucky for him, she let the matter drop. "Back to our

boss and the whole he-sucks-at-golf thing. How did this whole tournament come about anyhow? If he's so bad at golfing, and by all accounts, his brother sucks too, then why do they do keep at it?"

He shrugged. "Because they're males, and it beats the wars they used to indulge in to keep themselves entertained. Or so I've heard. Who cares? In a few days, it will be over, and I can go back to my life."

She said it before he could think it. "What life?"

"Are ye disparaging my lifestyle?"

"Oh please. You sat in a bar, for decades on end, getting dirty, hairy, and drunk. That's not living."

"As opposed to ye, Miss How-High-Can-I-Jump-Boss?" Yeah, he'd noticed how Aella, while sarcastic, made sure to stay on Lucifer's good side. She didn't take the same care with him, which for some reason, annoyed him.

"Hey, don't act pissy with me because I've got a job. Not all of us let one failed relationship turn us into a sobbing wreck bemoaning their fate."

"I didn't fail. She cheated."

"So what?"

So, it sucked. He answered another part of her accusation. "I do not bemoan."

"But you are a wreck."

Not anymore, he wanted to say. Yet, wasn't he planning to return to his old life in a few days? Well, his castle at least. He didn't think he'd be burying himself at the Triple D anytime soon. The dark locale had lost its appeal. "And what do ye suggest I do?"

She shrugged. "I don't know. Something. Anything."

"Work for Lucifer dragging back naughty demons and souls?"

"Nah. Not your style."

"Are ye saying I'm not good enough?"

"No. I know you can fight, but, you have to admit you don't take orders well. I'd say you're better suited being an entrepreneur."

"A what?"

"Own your own business. Do something you like."

"I like killing things." He especially wanted to decimate the vampire who'd turned around to take a second peek at the pert ass of his lass.

"You also enjoy playing golf."

"Do not."

"Whatever. Lie if you want. I saw your face when you held that club. You miss the game."

He did. More than he'd realized. "Maybe. But it also ruined my life."

"And here comes the woe-is-me bit again." She rolled her eyes. "Get the fuck over it. She screwed you over. You didn't like it. Boo-fucking-hoo. Welcome to Hell. It happened to me, too, but do you see me moping around? Nope. I'm out having fun. Getting my axe bloody. Making friends."

"Ye have friends?" He didn't mean for it to emerge sounding so incredulous.

"Ha ha, funny guy. And yes, I do. A couple, which is more than I can say for you."

True, damn her. They arrived in front of a bar, the raucous music and laughter within not appealing, nor was the thought of downing some fiery shots.

"Where would ye be right now if ye weren't babysitting me?"

"Me?" She shrugged. "Probably at home watching some television. Or out with a few of my friends."

"Doing?"

"I'd rather not say."

"Tell me."

"You'll laugh."

"I promise I won't. Scot's honor."

Her face scrunched up as if pained, and then she relaxed and sighed. "Okay, but keep in mind, you so much as let out one snort of amusement and you are dead." Still, she hesitated, even peeked around before she leaned in to whisper, "We go out and do karaoke."

He just about chuckled, but seeing her hand reaching for her axe, choked it back, especially as he realized she was serious. "No!"

"Yes, and if you tell a soul, I'll rip your dick off."

"But ye don't seem like the type."

She drew herself straight. "And what type is that?"

"I don't know. Ye are a hot, sexy woman. I just can't picture ye belting out the lyrics to 'I Will Survive.'"

"That's because I prefer to belt out eighties songs, or remakes of. I do a particularly great version of 'Sweet Dreams,' the Marilyn Manson version, of course."

"That I've got to see and hear. Where's the nearest karaoke place?"

"Excuse me?"

"Ye heard me, lass. Take me to your singing bar of choice. I want to hear ye using that throat for something other than gobbling."

Her nose wrinkled. "I do not gobble."

"Slurp then. Either way, it feels fucking fantastic. But we'll get to that later after ye dazzle me with your other vocal talents."

"What if I don't want to?"

"Then I'll make you sing soprano here on the street."

Her eyes narrowed. "You wouldn't."

"I'm a dirty ol' Scot, or so ye keep telling me." He leered and waggled his brows. "I would." And then kill anyone who watched because she wasn't the only one with jealousy issues. But he kept that tidbit to himself.

She relented quicker than expected. "Fine. I'll take you. But, I warn you, it's not your type of joint."

"If it serves alcohol, then I'll fit right in."

Or not, he revised when he entered the techno-colored, disco-ball lit blast from the seventies, replete with fake leather-covered stools, red Formica tables, and waitresses on roller skates bearing huge trays of drinks.

"So this is where the cast for *Happy Days* ended up," he muttered, feeling a little underdressed in his kilt and linen shirt, especially compared to the fellows in polyester suits with the fat lapels, ruffled shirtfronts, and shiny loafers. Not that he'd ever wear such a ridiculous getup. Perhaps he should have stuck to finding an establishment that played the bagpipes.

But then he wouldn't have seen Aella relax, her shoulders dropping from their usual tense pose, her head bopping in time to the music. And, good fucking grief, was that a bloody smile curling her lips? It was, and his undead heart stuttered. Looking younger than her years, Aella let the hint of the girl she once was peek through.

The grin on her face and the twinkle in her eyes captivated him, almost as much as her body, which jiggled as she found them a table. More like cleared one. She didn't even need to shed any blood. Unsheathing her axe did the trick. The patrons scattered, and before he'd even sat down, a waitress on wheels had wiped the table clean and popped out her notepad.

Chewing her gum a mile a minute, her hair upswept in a ponytail, the waitress looked perfectly innocent until you noticed her black orbs with no pupils and the tail peeking from beneath her poodle skirt. Succubus, he'd guess. With all the sexual energy running through this place, it made the most logical sense. "What will y'all have?"

"A lager for him." Aella waved in his direction. "And bring me a flaming inferno. Extra hot."

"Coming right up." With a snap of her gum, their waitress spun and whizzed off, weaving through the crowd on her wheels.

Leaning his elbows on the table, Niall stared at Aella, who returned his gaze without blinking. When the silence stretched too long, he finally caved and spoke first. "This place is a nightmare of epic proportions." He nearly died again when a giggle bubbled forth from her.

"Isn't it though? The first time Sasha and Katie dragged me here, I threatened to kill them both."

"I can see why."

"But then, they ordered some shooters, and the music ended up decent. Next thing I knew, we were singing some corny tune by Debbie Gibson and laughing our asses off. It was the most fun I'd had in ages."

"Sasha and Katie are?"

"My best friends. Sasha is a psychic, and Katie is a psycho."

"Excuse me, but I thought I heard you call your best friend a psycho."

"Yup, although having a boyfriend has mellowed her out and saved the bachelors who used to fuck her from an early demise."

"Where is that drink? I think I need an alcoholic buffer before I try to figure out what you're saying."

The waitress returned with their drinks, and Aella ordered them a second round before he'd even taken a sip from his first.

"Why, lass, if I didn't know any better, I'd think you're trying to get me drunk."

"I am. I figure that's the only way you're getting on stage to sing."

"I ain't singing."

Turned out that wasn't quite true. It took a copious amount of booze, lots of coaxing, the promise of a blowjob, and her going first—singing a cock-hardening version of 'Touch Me' by who-the-fuck-cared because it was hot—before he made it to the microphone. But once he got that little piece of plastic and wiring in his hand, Niall turned into a crooner. He belted out his version of 'Dead or Alive' to cheers and stomping feet and the smiling face of Aella, who clapped along and hooted encouragement, egging him on.

And damn it, she was right. It was fucking bloody fun.

11

AELLA COULDN'T HELP but watch her big Scot as he sang an atrocious rendition of what he claimed was the only decent song to emerge from the eighties. He massacred it. Killed it beyond all recognition, yet she'd never heard anything more wonderful. When was the last time she'd smiled so wide or had so much fun? *And because of a man.* Not just any man, but a Niall, an old-fashioned Scot with hidden layers, each more fascinating than the next.

Thank goodness for the alcohol that muddled her thought processes or she might have questioned her decision to pull down her toga and flash her tits at him while wolf whistling. His eyes flared red, his teeth popped out from under his top lip, and with a mighty leap, he came off the stage, his kilt fluttering and giving the ladies quite an eyeful.

Not that he paid any mind to the catcalls and invitations—Aella stored them and the faces behind them for later. Some bitches needed lessons in hitting on a lamia's man.

And he was her man. Her Scot. Her lover. *Mine.*

In all her centuries, Aella never recalled any male ever attracting, and, yes, even enchanting her like Niall did. Something about the wild vampire, with his throwback kilts and sexy brogue, didn't just make her panties wet; it did things to her heart. Made her feel things she'd thought long lost to her human days. He made her want. Want him. Want a forever fucking after.

Lucky for him she was drunk enough to not argue it, but not too far gone that it didn't frighten her a bit. Lust wiped the fear away when he pulled her into his arms for a deep kiss.

With the lights pulsing, the music pounding, and her heart racing, she let herself get swept up by the passion his mouth promised and allowed his hands to roam her body, raising her ardor to a fevered pitch, one that demanded instant satisfaction.

"I want ye," he growled in her ear before biting the lobe and sucking the sensitive tip.

"We're only a fifteen-minute walk from my place," she replied, arching to give him better access.

"Too far. Come with me." He gripped her hand in his and tugged her through the swaying bodies to the back of the room.

"Where are we going?" she queried.

"Somewhere a little more private," was his enigmatic reply.

His idea of private and hers differed. In he stalked to the female's washroom, his snapped, "Get out!" sending those at the sinks scurrying, most wearing knowing smirks. As for those in the stalls, a brisk pounding on the two locked doors had them flushing in a hurry.

Amusement cooling her ardor, Aella leaned back against the chipped porcelain sink and watched her Scot as he ushered the last female—a demon in heels almost as high as her legs—out the door. He slammed the portal shut and propped his frame against it. His eyes took on a smoldering intensity as he eyed her. He crooked a finger and beckoned.

She should have lopped it off for his temerity or flipped him a bird in reply, done anything but given in to his silent command with swaying hips. There was something oddly exciting about his impatience and the taboo location. There was just something irresistible about his crude charm.

Scorching lips found hers in a passionate kiss, which shot tingles from the tip of her head right down to her toes, and heat spread through her pussy. As his moist tongue tangled around hers, shudders wracked her body as need flared back to life even stronger than before.

Locked in a torrid embrace, they ignored the occasional pounding at the door. Their combined weight held those who attempted to enter at bay. The minor disturbances added to the moment, increasing the sense of urgency. Up came the hem of her toga as his hands roamed, caressing and igniting every nerve ending she possessed. The G-string she'd worn made him pause as his fingers skimmed over it.

"What's this? What happened to your usual attire? Or should I say lack of?"

She laughed. "Don't you like it?"

"Yes," he murmured, snapping the elastic, the sharp pinch making her jump. "But, again, why?"

"Because," she whispered in his ear, "I had a fantasy of you taking it off with your teeth."

And she had. But even her vivid imagination couldn't have imagined the erotic reality of it. He spun her so fast she almost lost her balance, but the door provided a steadying influence as he swapped their positions so she leaned against the portal. His hands bracketed either side of her hips to keep his weight holding it shut. Then with his lips and teeth alone, he nudged his way up her toga, the rough edge of his unshaven jaw tickling the skin of her thigh. From under the fabric, he paused then chuckled. "What's this? A gun?"

"Shotgun," she corrected. "For the times when just an axe won't do." It was a short-barreled, pump-action, acid-pellet toy, which she'd thought to bring along when she quickly hit her apartment to change before joining her Scot on his golfing lesson with Lucifer.

"Ye are just full of surprises," he murmured, kissing the skin in between the holster straps.

"I'd rather be full of you."

He groaned, the rumble of his reply on her flesh drawing forth an answering shudder. Up crept his lips, closer and closer to the source of her heat.

"Ye are so fucking sexy."

Words shouldn't have the ability to make a woman cream herself almost to the point of coming, but Aella still found her channel clenching tight, and her erratic pulse raced even faster. "Would you stop teasing me, Scot, and touch me already?"

Again, he laughed, a soft, low sound that quivered against the damp crotch of her panties. She dug her nails into his shoulders. She had to because her legs trembled, threatening to collapse.

His teeth tugged at the fabric covering her sex, and when they didn't budge, he tore them from her, drawing forth a small cry as the cooler air tickled her feverish flesh. Then his lips pressed against her, and heat exploded as his tongue swirled in wet circles around her engorged clit.

"Oh. Oh. Oh." Already, she stood poised on the brink of climax, which was what made the intrusion at that crucial moment so fucking rude.

"There he is. Kill him." The guttural command, male in origin and out of place, snapped her eyes open. Even gripped in the throes of passion, she possessed enough wits to know her orgasm would have to wait. Apparently, Niall came to that same conclusion as he pulled himself with reluctance from his enjoyable feast. Holy fuck, did he look pissed.

It seemed that, despite the threat to his person, only an idiot should get in between a vampire and his erotic dinner.

They should have also known better than to interrupt a lamia's climax.

As Niall stood and whipped around to face the demons who appeared in the washroom, the five portals that materialized allowing them entry, Aella straightened, and her toga fell to cover her pulsing—and none too happy at the delay—lower parts.

"Who wants to die first?" snarled her equally irritated Scot.

The five brutes facing them just grinned in reply and took a step forward as one unit. So Aella made the choice for them. Drawing her shotgun, she took aim and fired.

It didn't decapitate her choice, not like her trusty axe, but a face full of acid pellets had the brutish-appearing thug screaming and clawing at his skin. It also got the action started. With a battle cry to rival that of Mel Gibson's in *Braveheart*, Niall charged, his sword sheathed at his side as he relied on his bare hands and teeth to do his work. In the close confines of the bathroom, Aella found it more difficult to wield her axe, mostly because, for once, she didn't fight alone. Usually, she would have hacked and slashed her way to victory, but given she wanted Niall intact, she needed to temper her wild swings. Not that he needed her help.

It seemed a horny vampire was more than a match for an attacking squad of goons. With a speed only vampires possessed, and a violent nature not afraid to shed some blood, break some bones, or tear off limbs, Niall made quick work of the interruption, snapping necks and ripping out pulsing, black hearts.

It was effective, yet quite messy, not to mention a mood breaker, especially since they no longer blocked the doorway and a crowd of females had pushed their way into the bathroom. Some ignored the carnage and went about their feminine business. Others, though... Others gawked at her Scot. One brazen hussy even ran a finger down his muscled arm and licked the blood off the tip. Aella gave her something to suck when she lopped off the offending digit.

Before Aella could get embroiled in a riot with the female patrons who took offense at her jealous action, Niall snagged her around the waist and upended her over his wide shoulder, carting her out of the bar to the catcalls of the male patrons. Aella allowed it because, honestly, what else could they do? They'd lost their sex spot, she didn't feel like singing, and she could think of better things to do than kill the females ogling her Scot.

Especially when Niall muttered something about getting her in a shower and continuing where they'd left off.

"You can put me down now," she said after he'd walked a few blocks.

"Why?"

"So I can walk."

"But I like ye where ye are," he replied, the arm banded across her thighs tightening.

"Where are you taking me?"

"Somewhere with a bed."

"Shouldn't we be instead reporting the attack to Lucifer?"

"Bah. That wasn't an attack."

"Tell that to the bodies we left behind."

"If they were serious about taking me out, they would have sent more," he boasted. "That was just a wee warning."

"Which I take it hasn't deterred you from acting as our lord's caddy and teacher."

He snorted. "On the contrary. Now I want the devil to win. Anyone willing to insult me by sending less than their best to kill me deserves to get spanked by the worst golfer alive."

She couldn't help but snicker. "You are evil."

"Says the lass who goes around with a shotgun strapped to her thigh and an axe on her back."

"In my line of work, it pays to be prepared."

It also paid to have a letter from Lucifer entitling the bearer to demand free accommodations at any establishment in Hell. Niall strode into the first hotel they came across, a ritzy place despite its location in the fourth circle and, in short order, had them ensconced in a penthouse suite, naked, and in a shower of epic proportions.

She expected him to resume his erotic tease of before, but instead, he washed her with sure, quick strokes. Mind, those skimming hands covered in suds still had her body humming and her pussy craving, but his lips didn't so much as give her a single lick.

She couldn't help but pout when he toweled her dry.

"What's with the face?" he asked as he knelt on one knee, patting her skin with the fluffy fabric. "Ye look so disappointed."

"What happened to taking up where we left off?" No point in beating around the bush. Coyness was for virgins and annoying bitches. Both were the type Aella liked to kill.

"Is someone feeling neglected?" he teased as he picked up her foot to dry the bottom.

"Yes."

He laughed, a wicked rumble that shot a shiver down

her spine. "Never fear, lass. I'm not done with ye. I just thought I'd get ye nice and clean first for the dirty things I have planned."

Hmm, that sounded promising.

"Ye aren't the only one with a fantasy," he admitted as he stood and towered over her, his blue eyes blazing.

"What's yours? And if you tell me it involves sheep, I'm out of here."

His laughter boomed, and she smiled along with him. "Lass, ye are a treasure. Come with me, and I'll show ye."

The suite he'd booked contained a bed, a really large bed, with a soft, plushy comforter that cushioned her back when he tossed her upon it. She bounced. He pounced. And she stretched sinuously under his naked body.

"I'm clean. We found the bed. Now what?" she asked with an arched brow. "Does your fantasy involve cuffs? Syrup? I don't see mirrors on the ceiling."

"That's a different fantasy, lass. This one involves your legs over my shoulders."

"Like this?" She pointed her toes as she brought her legs up to rest on his skin. His eyes turned dark and smoldering.

"Aye. Like that." It also apparently involved him giving her the best cunnilingus of her life until she screamed his name as she dug her heels into his back. But tonguing her wasn't the only thing he'd dreamed of.

He'd no sooner brought her pussy back to a fevered state, slick and trembling, than he flipped her onto her stomach, propping her ass up as he did.

Exposed to his gaze, she couldn't help but peek over

her shoulder as he rubbed the tip of his dick at the entrance of her sex. "Admiring the view?" she asked.

"Aye."

"I'd prefer you fucked it."

"I will." Back and forth he teased her.

She shook her hips, but he didn't take her up on her silent invitation. "I'm waiting."

"I know."

Smug bastard. "Would you hurry up already?"

"Fuck me, lass. Must ye always have the last word?"

"Yes. Got a problem with that?"

He growled. "No, which I don't get. I'm the man."

"And?"

"I should give the orders."

"Let me guess? I should accept them meekly with my head bowed? Don't be so old fashioned."

"Can I help it if, in my time, women were seen not heard?"

"Don't forget, I remember that time. I wasn't born yesterday, you know. But I've adapted. Matured and found a spine. I've lived long enough to know what I want and am not afraid to ask for it."

"And what do ye want?"

She wiggled her ass. "For you to stop teasing me with that big cock of yours and fuck me already. Or do I need to finish the job myself?" In case he didn't get her hint, she reached between her legs and rubbed a finger over her clit, using her own juices as lube before flicking the head of his shaft.

With a mangled cry, he slammed into her, each thrust

accompanied by curt words. "Ye." Slam. "Are driving me." Pull out. "Fucking." Driving back. "Insane."

Funny, she could have said the same as she clawed at the bedding, each stroke and grunted expression bringing her pleasure higher and higher. It amused her to know her forthrightness frustrated him. It turned her on to see him succumb despite it.

Back and forth he thrust, murmuring endearments one moment, cursing his lack of control at others until, with a mighty cry, he spilled inside her, the hot gush of liquid making her tight channel spasm and milk his spurting length.

As usual after one of their rough couplings, he collapsed atop her, but before she could complain, he rolled them and placed her on his chest. Lying atop him, skin on skin and panting, Aella relaxed as an almost peaceful haze drifted over her. His hand stroked her cheek, and she curled into it, the intimacy not something she ever indulged in. With him, though, she craved it. She closed her eyes as he spoke to her in his sexy brogue.

"You are so fucking beautiful."

"I'm sure you say that to all the ladies."

"Nay. Just ye. Only ye. Damn ye for making me feel again."

Feel? Was he admitting he cared for her? As in more than just a fuck buddy or cover for her job as his body-guard? What did he mean? Dare she ask? Or should she just kill him? And how did she feel? She opened her mouth to ask him to explain, but his soft snore clamped it shut.

He fell asleep! She opened her eyes and canted her head to look. Indeed, the man who'd just dropped a verbal bomb snoozed, mouth open, eyes closed, hair standing on end, looking innocent and all male at the same time. She didn't know if she should slap him awake or kiss him goodnight.

She did neither, but when she went to slide off his body, the arms looped loosely around her tightened, and trapped in his embrace, she slipped into dreamland where, instead of razing the castle with the princess to the ground, she was the one high in the tower while Niall rode in on a black charger, tartan fluttering, slaying the prince who stood in his way so he could kidnap and then ravish her. She'd never had a better night's sleep.

1 2

NIALL FEIGNED slumber as soon as he realized he'd slipped and told her more than he'd meant to. What was he thinking? Admitting to Aella he had feelings for her was suicide in more than a few ways. One, it gave her the power to hurt him. Hurt, use, and destroy him because he doubted he'd recover this time round if Aella betrayed him. Two, even if he could trust her, which more and more he suspected he could, she also had issues when it came to feelings and commitment. Did he want to wake up minus some body parts or, worse, not wake up at all? He'd gotten a glimpse at how Aella dealt with her emotions. Nothing much tended to survive.

Fuck did he like that about her.

He liked too many things, and it was a problem he intended to avoid as long as he could. He spent a restless night, his body a pillow for the vixen who vexed him, his mind a whirl as it spent one moment imagining a future with her then the next destroying it with how it would feel if she didn't return his affections and tore out his newly beating heart.

The lack of sleep and angst made him particularly testy the following day on the barren golf course where the Lord of Sin proved he was Master of the Mulligan.

Lucifer whacked at the golf ball, the head hitting it slightly off center, sending the missile on a curved path. It landed, just like the previous fifty shots, in the sand trap with a puff of flying dust.

"I fucking hate this game," the Lord of the Underworld snarled as another club went flying. And again, as with previous club launches hurled in anger, something yelped in the distance. Why Lucifer's tantrum aim was so good when his intentional ones always ended up so bad was something Niall didn't have the inclination to dwell on, not today, not with Aella giving him the cold shoulder since she'd woken that morning.

"And the game hates ye right back," Niall snapped, his eyes hidden by sunglasses to camouflage not only his sleepless state, but the fact he couldn't keep his eyes from following Aella's every move.

"I need a drink," Satan groused.

"What ye need to do is concentrate on what I'm telling ye."

"It's not fucking working."

"Because ye are not bloody listening," Niall roared. "So stop your bitching and moaning and get your hairy arse in that pit with a fucking sand wedge and get the ball out, which I might remind, ye put there."

"What if I don't want to? Maybe I want to leave the damned thing there."

"Stop acting like a whining, panty-wearing princess and fix your mistake. Maybe if ye get some sand up your arse crack and chafe, ye'll stop hitting it there in the first place."

"Anyone ever mention you suck as a teacher?"

"Cry me a fucking river. Perhaps ye should switch to playing Barbies and leave the real sports to the big boys," Niall taunted right back.

The flipped finger made Niall's lips curl at the corner. But their verbal sparring had the desired effect. The Lord of Sin, face set in a scowl, stomped off to hit his buried ball.

Niall's grin widened.

"You're having fun," Aella accused in a low tone, finally deigning to speak to him after hours of silence.

"Of course I am. It's not every day a man gets to tell one of the most powerful beings ever what to do and mock him while doing it."

"You're evil."

"And ye have been avoiding me." He took his snake by the tail and shook her, tired of the strained silence between them.

"Am not."

He took a step toward her, and she took an automatic one back.

"Are too. Care to tell me why?"

"Just doing what I'm paid for and keeping an eye out for trouble."

"Ye and I both know that's a lie. Something is bothering ye."

"Would you stop asking me questions? What I feel is none of your business."

"I say it is."

"No, it's not, or have you forgotten this whole dating thing is a sham. You're not my real boyfriend. We have nothing."

"Bullshit. What we have is more than a mission."

She wouldn't look him in the eye, but she did lick her full lips. "No, it isn't. You're just a job, one that ends after the match tomorrow."

"Is that all I am to ye?" As usual when his emotions ran high, his brogue emerged thicker than usual. "A job?"

"Of course. What else did you expect?"

"I hoped ye wouldn't lie."

"What do you want from me?"

"More than ye are apparently willing to give. And more than I should expect."

"What did you expect?"

Good question. But he knew he wanted more than for her to see him as just a job. *I want her to see me as a man. See me as her lover. Her future.* What happened to never trusting or loving again? Great vows for a past so far gone he couldn't even recall the color of Fionnaghal's eyes. But he knew that of Aella's—yellow with the narrowest of slits when she was angry, glowing golden with wide black bands when she was amused, and black bottomless orbs when she was on the verge of coming and screaming his name.

"Well, Scot? What do you want from me other than protection and a hole to dip your cock?"

Your love. He bit his tongue, but her crossed arms and tense expression demanded a reply. "Forget I asked. For some reason, I thought we could continue seeing each other once this was all over. Guess I was mistaken. Blame it on my age and old-fashioned views."

Her mouth opened and then shut, and her face went through a myriad of expressions, but in the end, she never expressed any of the thoughts running through her head because Lucifer, of course, ruined the moment with his shouted, "Fuck me to the Milky Way and back. I got the little bastard out and on the green. And it only took me five strokes this time. I think I'm getting better."

The Lord of Sin might have finally shaved a few strokes off his game, but Niall felt like he'd lost a prime opportunity with Aella. Citing some lame excuse about seeing a psychic friend in need, his lass scurried off after assigning some area guards to watch over them.

Grabbing a club, Niall cursed and whacked at the whip-thin brush dotting the edge of the putting area.

"And I thought my swing was off," Lucifer remarked as he leaned on his putter, watching. "Want to talk about what's bothering you?"

"As if ye fucking care."

"I do actually because if your head's not in the game, then you're not giving me your hundred and one percent. Which means my game is at risk. And we can't have that. The world revolves around me, you know. So get your head out of your ass and focus back on the most important thing here. Me."

But Niall couldn't. "I don't understand her. I could have sworn she felt something for me."

"Who says she doesn't?"

"Aella, of course. She says I'm just a job."

"And you believe her?"

"Why wouldn't I? She's the one who constantly claims she's not afraid to speak her mind. That she's a modern woman."

Smoke blew out of the devil's nose. "You are such an idiot. Anyone can see the gal is nuts about you. Or do you think she screws all her missions?"

"How the fuck would I know? I never asked." Because he feared going on a murderous rampage if she did tell him about past lovers. His jealousy knew no bounds where she was concerned.

"The answer is no. Nor does she take them to her favorite karaoke bar. Or spend the night with them. Or cause thousands in damages at brothels chasing them down. Aella is usually a very composed minion. If something pisses her off, or confuses her, she kills it."

"I still don't get it."

"You, my kilted caddy, are still very much alive, or is that undead? Even I'm not sure what the politically correct term is anymore for your kind. Not that I give a fuck. You still have a head on your shoulders and are still mobile despite the fact you wiggled your way under her skin. She must like you."

"Well, she has a funny way of showing it."

"What did you expect? Fucking flowers and poetry? She's a hunter. A demon. A woman used to getting her way and showing no vulnerability."

"And I'm a warrior."

"As well as a stubborn ass. One of you needs to bend and say something first or you'll both end up alone. Is that what you want?"

Live without his lass? Go back to his barren existence? He swung and hit the ball on the ground with a solid thunk. It soared through the air and landed with a swish in the cup.

Lucifer whistled. "Fuck me. If only you could play in my place."

"So ye think I need to tell her how I feel?"

"No. But I'll bet it's what she wants. I know Gaia is always asking me to tell her how much I care. You'd think the fact I swore off other women would be enough. But no. She likes me to say it out loud. Damned emasculating, if you ask me."

Niall knew well the embarrassment. He'd suffered through it once before. "Last time I was open with my heart, I got screwed."

"By a woman you'd barely spoken two words to the entire time you knew her. This time round, you've had time to get to know her. What does your gut say?"

His gut? How about his heart? It screamed she cared. It insisted he trust. It begged him not to let fear and pride stand in the way of claiming his demon. "I preferred the old days when we just traded cows and gold for our brides. This talking shit is annoying."

"Tell me about it. Who knew when I told that female to eat that damned apple the havoc it would cause."

Then again, would Niall love Aella as much if she didn't have such a sharp mind and tongue? Not that he

127

got to tell her that night. Citing a need for Niall to be rested and not all sexed out, Lucifer placed him in lockdown. No Aella. No booze. No nothing. Thank fuck for the lotion in the bathroom and his hand. Given how he couldn't get his mind off Aella, he might have died of frustration otherwise.

1 3

Aella slammed into Sasha's shop practically hyperventilating. She'd run from the golf course to her friend's place, her talk with Niall sending her into a panic. Unable to deal with it and needing some advice without him distracting her, she'd gone to the one person she trusted.

Sporting large hoop earrings and enough chains to sink a ship, Sasha barely glanced up from behind the counter. She did however say, "Yes, you are being a big fucking chicken."

As usual, Sasha already knew the cause of her angst. Having a psychic as a BFF really helped cut a lot of the bullshit. "I can't help it. He wants us to have a relationship. I think he might even be—" She dropped her voice to a low whisper. "In love with me."

"And?"

"What do you mean and? What am I supposed to do?" Cut off his head? Stake him? Run for the hills?

"Um, why not love him back?"

"But he's—he's—"

"Hot."

How dare her friend notice! "Yes, but—"

"Violent."

Which she liked. "Yes, but —"

"Willing to put up with your shit."

"Again, yes, but —"

"Would you stop with the fucking buts? You love him. Stop finding stupid excuses and admit it."

Her first instinct was deny, deny, deny. But lying to her BFF was wrong. "Fine. I do love him. I don't understand why, but I do. However, we can't be together." The exact reason why wasn't entirely clear to her, but centuries of shunning relationships held sway.

"Why the heck not?"

Well, she could think of at least one valid point. "He thinks women should be meek little creatures who look pretty and don't have an opinion."

"Does he? And yet he's fallen for the most loud-mouthed bitch I know."

"I am not a bitch."

"Okay Ms. Has-To-Have-The- Last-Word."

"It's called confidence."

"If you say so. And look at that, despite the fact you have an abundance of *confidence,* he still wants you for more than just a hole to screw. He also talks to you. Listens to you. Thinks you're cute when you're chopping the heads off demons. Wants to kill anything that covets you."

Oh, how adorable. She wanted to kill those coveting him too. "He loves me." It finally hit her. Truly sank in, along with wonderment and a warmth not related to Hell's infernal heat.

"Give the snake a mouse. Yes, he loves you. As you are, and despite his old-fashioned views. Just like you love him. So would you stop being scared?"

"What if it doesn't work out?"

"Then you'll survive. But that won't be a problem. Don't forget, I see the future."

"And?"

"Trust me when I say if you make the right choice now, you have centuries of disgusting happiness ahead of you."

She did? Then what was she waiting for? "I should go back to him."

"You should. But not until morning."

Mind made up, Aella's impatience struck. "Why not?"

"Lucifer has him under lock and key with strict orders not to let anyone in. He's not taking any chances with his caddy with the match happening tomorrow. You'll have to wait."

Wait. But she wanted to see him now. Thankfully, Sasha, having foreseen her disappointment, had stocked up on ice cream and girly flicks. It wasn't a night spent in her Scot's arms, but at least she didn't mope alone.

THE DAY of the tournament dawned grey and ashy, in Hell at least. Out upon the mortal plane, in the wilds of the Australian outback where the tourney was being held, the sun blazed as it rose over the horizon, promising heat and cloudless conditions, or so Mother Earth claimed.

At the first hole, the participants and their caddies lined up.

God, with his archangel Raphael as his caddy, dressed all in whites from their collared shirts to their Bermuda shorts and cleated shoes. Even the golf bag, made of synthetic white fibers, shone in the dawning glare.

Zeus, wearing his customary toga, a light blue with a golden sash that matched his gold-trimmed bag, stood stroking his beard while his caddy, Hermes, struggled under his load, muttering about the indignity of being a ball carrier.

The Lord of Limbo, featureless and dressed in a cowled gray robe, stood still as a statue, the fabric of his clothing fluttering in a wind that only seemed to affect him while his bag hovered by his side. His caddy, a sexless, wraithlike being, while humanoid in shape, was alien at the same time, with pupil-less eyes and only a seamless expanse where his mouth should have been.

The fourth in the group was none other than the Lord of the Pit himself—or as HBC stated in their live report, *"Rounding out the quartet is our very own lord of despair, the king of all sin, the ultimate fornicator, the biggest, baddest devil ever to play...".* Resplendent in another eye-popping outfit, Lucifer wore flame-patterned shorts, a vivid red shirt, black shoes, and a smirk. Niall, the bag slung over his shoulder and wearing his usual plaid and linen shirt—as well as sunblock specially made for vampires, SPF 666— wanted to roll his eyes as Lucifer waved and played to the thick crowd of spectators. He had to hand it to the powerful demon. He knew how to work people into an excited frenzy.

Their foursome wasn't the only one to compete. A few other deities rounded out the two other groups, but none really worth noting, not with Satan stealing the show.

When Gaia stepped daintily from the crowd, a vision of springtime loveliness in her gauzy green gown and hair crowned in a wreath of flowers, the crowd stamped and whistled, especially when Lucifer spun her and dipped her for a long kiss.

Cheeks flushed, eyes bright, and giggling, she waved to her lover before skipping back while Lucifer leered at her and commented on those within hearing—"Damned fine woman. I can't wait to claim my victory BJ when this is over." It didn't even faze him when the bolt of lightning struck out of nowhere and left his hair standing on end. Zeus peered at his hand then the sky, brow beetling, while Gaia glared.

It didn't take a genius to figure out who'd taken offense at his words.

But who cared when a blow of trumpets, a whole angelic choir of them, sounded? The tournament—and torture—began.

Balls went flying, not always in the right direction. It was painful to watch, and yet watch everyone did, not for the sport itself, but for the underlying politics as deities were forced to spend time in each other's company.

Lucifer especially enjoyed himself.

"Zeus, old man, I see you got the beard untangled from your latest lover's snatch. You should ask your barber next time you see him to give you a Brazilian." The crowed tittered, especially since the Greek god clearly didn't understand the reference.

"Limbo, or may I call you Limbless? How on earth do you get oral if your minions don't have mouths?" That question went viral on Twitpit as everyone speculated on if the sealed upper lips also meant sealed lower ones.

"Hey, big brother, nice parasol. Did you steal it from my girlfriend?" A frothy white concoction, it shaded God from the burning sun. He didn't do well in the heat, a fact Lucifer mocked him for loudly and often, comparing his reddening skin to that of a lobster. The religious in the crowd began muttering, and Niall could already predict Hell would acquire some new souls as previously pristine Heavenly inhabitants accidentally sinned in their outrage.

On and on, the taunting went, throwing the players off

their game, which in turn helped Lucifer, who sucked as usual. It was a long fucking morning, made longer by the fact Niall could see Aella in the crowd; he just couldn't touch or talk to her.

Despite how she'd run off the day before, she seemed happy to see him today, or at least so he assumed by her wave and smile when their eyes first met. He did wonder, though, why she kept biting her lower lip, looking worried. He intended to find out as soon as this match from Hell ended. Which, at the rate things were going, would take all bloody day.

As the sun blazed down, hotter and hotter, sweat trickled down the crease of his spine. It was about as attractive as it sounded, so when Lucifer hit a ball in the woods, Niall almost cheered because the shade of the boughs was a welcome relief.

"How am I doing?" the devil asked as they trudged across the sandy fairway to the shadowy copse.

"Pretty good considering." And he was. Whether it was dumb luck or just the other players having a shitty day, they were all within a few strokes of each other, nobody really leading the pack in any way, and getting close to the end with only a half dozen more holes to go.

"Yeah, what a stroke of luck when that vulture scooped that Limbo dude's ball as it flew by," Lucifer remarked with a smug smile.

"Is that what they call it nowadays?"

"Why, Niall, are you accusing me of cheating?" Affront on Satan's face proved a comical thing to see.

"As if." Niall snorted. "Just saying it was mighty convenient considering it would have put him ahead three strokes on that hole."

"One can't control the forces of nature," Lucifer replied gravely.

"But one can fuck it until she screams with pleasure," he muttered back.

"Yes. Yes, one can. What can I say? When I do that trick where I swirl my hips…" Lucifer demonstrated, and Niall nearly walked into a tree, his temporary blindness to blame.

Under the relative coolness of spindly branches, they stopped speaking as they hunted for the elusive white ball. They'd left the cheering and jeering of the crowd behind, the only noise that of their feet crunching the fallen branches and detritus of a forest left to its own natural devices.

The attack took them both by surprise, especially since it came from above and without warning. From the trees dropped dozens of giant spiderlike bodies, the multi-jointed legs and huge segmented bodies reminiscent of the earth variety, if they came in nuclear-induced sizes bigger than his fist and a vivid neon pink. How they'd managed to camouflage themselves Niall didn't have time to ponder, not when they seemed intent on swarming him to sink their dripping, probably venomous, quad of fangs into him.

"What in hell are these?" he yelled.

"Not from Hell, that's for sure," Lucifer stated. "These suckers aren't from any of the planes I've visited."

"What do we do?" Niall asked, shaking a few critters free and booting them.

"Kill them, of course."

Not having brought his sword—the tourney supposed to be weapons-free and neutral of conflict—Niall did the next best thing. He pulled out a number seven iron and began to whack at them.

"Take that, you bloody bastard," he cursed as a hairy pink body went flying to splat against a gnarly tree bole. "And that. And that." Again and again, he swung, each swing of the club sending a nasty critter flying, his aim unerring.

As for Lucifer, he crowed as he swirled, aiming his finger in a gunlike motion and shouting, "Bang, you're dead." Of course, instead of bullets, he shot out balls of flame, but they still did the trick, igniting the alien invaders and burning them to a crisp, the acrid stench not entirely unpleasant and reminding him he'd yet to have lunch.

In the midst of their arachnid battle, Aella appeared, a grimace on her face. "Eew. Figures. I hate spiders."

"How did you know to come find us?" Niall asked in between swings.

"Call it instinct. That and the rather obvious distraction on the golf course. It's raining purple daisies, so Zeus is calling foul on Mother Nature, who, in turn, is claiming a frame job. Meanwhile, no one seems to have noticed you both disappeared and haven't returned. I got suspicious so I thought I'd wander away while no one was watching and check in on you."

"Ye shouldn't have. Ye'll get dirty," Niall replied in an attempt at chivalry.

Dressed as the girlfriend of a participant, which

meant short skirt, tight blouse, and impractical shoes, she didn't have much to offer as a shield or weapon. Niall moved to place himself in front of her as a line of defense.

As if she'd allow that. She sidestepped him and peered down at the skittering critters with a moue of distaste. "Damn it all. Security took my sword and my gun," she grumbled as she stomped on one with her shoe, the squishing sound not as gross as the squelched guts between her sandaled toes.

Lucifer paused his fireball flinging to give her hell. "You're not supposed to be here. Rules state only the players, caddy, or game officials can be present on the course."

"Since when do you follow rules?"

Satan shrugged. "Just making sure you're breaking the rules on purpose so I can add a bonus to your paycheck later. Now do you mind earning that paycheck? We could use a little help."

A little indeed. But, just as Niall meant to ask how Lucifer thought she could help without any weapons, a forked tongue came flicking out of nowhere. Whirling, Niall beheld a disturbing sight. Aella had finally shifted over to her lamia shape, which meant her top half, still wearing the black blouse and white pearls, was human, while her bottom half sat in a coiled, sinuous heap, the tip of her tail rattling ominously. Out came her tongue, intriguingly long, split, and agile enough to snag another alien spider. For a moment, he feared she'd eat it, but no, she tossed it behind her where her tail, sporting some wicked barbs, lashed the spinning arachnid, skewering it into pieces.

"Lass, that is oddly hot," he told her as he sent a few more flying to meet their maker.

"You're sick, Scot."

"I must be because, no matter how ye treat me and ignore me and surprise me, I can't help but want and like ye."

"You do?" She paused in her spider killing to regard him.

"Of course I do."

"Well, you never actually said so."

"Did I not come with ye to see the idiot in the pompom over there?"

"Hey," Lucifer shouted. "I resent that. It's not a pompom but a tam."

"You didn't have a choice."

He snorted. "Love, if I'd not wanted to spend more time with ye, I could have disappeared in the wilds, and not ye or any other tracker would have found me."

"Which is why you went running to a whorehouse the first chance you got."

"And ended up proving to myself that ye were more than just a hot pussy. Ye mean something to me, lass." But apparently, he'd have to prove it.

"You dumped me on my ass after sex."

"Because caring for ye scared me."

"You said we were just pretending to be dating so I could protect you."

"So I could keep ye close to me."

"You sold your soul to win that Scottish bitch."

"I also killed her, her family, and laid waste to a decent portion of Scotland when she betrayed me."

"Gee, that makes me feel so much better."

"Ask me what I'd do if ye ever broke my trust or didn't want me back."

"What would you do?"

"Jump in the abyss and hope to never be reborn again. I don't want to keep living, or not living I should say, without ye. Before I met ye, I was waiting for the courage to die. Now I want to live, but only if ye are at my side. The question is, will ye?"

"Will I what?"

"Marry me, of course. Be the queen of my castle. The proud wearer of my plaid. The one to feed me when I hunger, and not just for blood. For everything. Love, sex, companionship. I want ye to be the one. My one."

"You're asking an awful lot. What do I get out of this?"

"Ye want more? I'm giving you my heart. My love. My loyalty and my life. What more do you want?"

She knew the answer to that one thanks to Sasha. "I want forever."

"Done."

"Oh no we're not," Lucifer snapped as he fried a final pink monstrosity. "Thanks for nothing. While you've been spewing lovey-dovey garbage, I had to protect myself."

"From teeny tiny bugs," Gaia mocked as she appeared out of nowhere. "Really, Lucifer. Did you have to make such a mess of my forest?"

"Well excuse me for trying to save my own skin."

"I guess I can forgive you this one time. But now would you stop dilly-dallying and get that ball moving? The game officials have noticed your absence and are heading this way, which means Aella and I need to scatter.

Come along, dear. Oh, and don't forget to put back on your bottom half. We wouldn't want any snake hunters to get any ideas. Your reptile coloring is quite striking and would make a beautiful purse and shoes. Ever think of selling your skin when you shed it?"

As the ladies winked out discussing the possibilities of starting a lamia line of leather products, Niall blinked. "Did I just imagine that conversation, or did she just say she'd be mine forever?"

"No hallucinations. Yet. The day is only half over, though, and you never know what interesting herbs we might run across."

Shit. Way to remind him they had six more holes to go before he could track Aella down and get her to repeat what she'd said. Way too long the way Lucifer played. Watching the demon, tongue peeking between his teeth as he swung and missed at his ball in the scrubby grass, he sighed.

"Move aside for a second, would ye?" Snagging the club from Lucifer's hand, Niall put himself in position.

"What? You? Cheating?" Lucifer staggered and clutched at his chest.

Drama king. "Ye can pay me a bonus later, preferably in stone and laborers so I can build my lass a bigger castle. Now shut up while I get ye going in the right direction." With a well-aimed swing, Niall sent the ball soaring before handing Lucifer back the club. Just in time, too, as game officials came trotting into sight.

With no witnesses, and the king of lies spinning an elaborate tale about attacking arachnids, no one could say a thing about the ball, which in a miracle, ended up not only clearing the copse but landing two feet from the cup. Even the devil would have had to work hard to miss that simple putt.

And so they played the rest of the game. Lucifer missing, and sending the ball often careening out of sight of cameras and crowd, and Niall quickly getting the ball back into play in a favorable position, until they were at the final hole.

God and the Devil were tied for first place, the other competitors having had unfortunate mishaps, one which might have proven fatal to the Lord of Limbo, who fell into a sand trap. The giant worm that emerged snapping him up whole was apparently not indigenous to the area or the planet. But hey, those were the risks they took when they signed up for the challenge.

Unfortunately, Niall couldn't help the lord of the pit with this final shot in full view of the crowd. As if sensing his impending victory, his ball sitting only ten feet from the cup, God couldn't help taunting his brother, which for those new to their relationship meant he was being stupidly nice and encouraging.

"You can do it, little brother. I know you can. Let's share this victory just like we share the same blood. Or is it essence?" God rubbed his chin. "Whatever it is that makes us family, know that I love you no matter what happens. Win or lose, we have each other."

Lucifer growled.

"Ignore him," Niall admonished. "He's just trying to throw off your game. Ye can do this. Ye are only twenty feet from the hole."

"Might as well be a hundred. We both know my putting skills suck."

Yeah, but his angry aim was never off. Niall had an idea, a long shot, but given the odds they faced now and their inability to cheat with the cameras and the eyes of the crowd on them, maybe it was their only choice.

He leaned in and whispered, "If ye don't win this, your minions will mock ye." Lucifer scowled. Niall murmured some more. "Gazillions are watching, waiting for ye to fuck up." Lucifer rumbled in discontent. Niall dropped the bomb, a fake one, but times called for drastic measures. "I hear Gaia's been fucking your brother behind your back and claiming his bigger dick is more satisfying than yours. As a matter of fact, the only reason she's still with ye is so she could spy and tell your brother about all your plans, usually while she's sucking his cock."

With smoke pouring from his ears, flames spewing from his nose, and his eyes burning like supernovas, Lucifer lost it. His club went swinging, bonked God upside the head, clipped Niall on the way, bounced back, and tapped the little benign golf ball on the ground.

As the dimpled sphere went rolling, Niall locked the devil in a headlock before he could go charging after his dazed brother, quickly saying in his ear, "I lied. Gaia never touched your brother."

Lucifer stilled. "She didn't?"

"Nope."

"So I don't get to kill the annoying goody two-shoes?"

"Why bother when you can humiliate him on the course? Look."

Look indeed. While Niall quickly worked to calm the Lord of Sin, a miracle happened. He sank his putt.

Lucifer quickly grasped what it meant. "If he misses, I win!"

Sensing the lord of the pit's change in mood, Niall released him, and Lucifer stood with his shoulders back, lips curved in a smirk, slicking back his hair and straightening his clothes.

Just as his brother prepared to putt, Lucifer—not one to leave things to chance—muttered under his breath, "I love you, big brother."

Of all the things he could have done, that probably ranked as the most startling. God, thrown off balance, bobbled his shot. The ball wobbled a few feet then stopped shy of the hole, placing Lucifer solidly in first place.

At first, the crowd remained silent, all eyes locked on the unfolding drama in disbelief. Then a wild roar rocked the barren plain as Hell's minions went wild. Fireballs flews, the earth shook, fists pumped in excitement, and a little blood was shed. All in all, as victories went, it was a relatively damage-free one.

As the angels sulked off, their billowy white wings drooping, and Limbo's spirits dissipated, indifferent to the result, and the Greeks yelled for retribution, as well as challenges, which went for the most part ignored, Lucifer chuckled.

"Damn it, Scot. That was fucking brilliant. But how did you know it would work?"

Niall shrugged. "I didn't. However, I did know I had to try something, and given ye couldn't soft putt if your life depended on it, I decided to use your freaky good aim when ye get truly pissed to good use."

"Don't think this victory means I'm tearing up your contract," Lucifer replied with narrowed eyes. "Your soul still belongs to me."

"But his heart and body are mine," Aella announced, coming up behind them. "That is if you were serious?"

Whirling around, he spied her upheld axe as she waited for his answer. A great big laugh made him shake. "Oh lass. Ye are a never-ending source of joy. Would ye truly decapitate me?"

"In a second. I won't ever let you go, Scott. If I give you my heart, you'd better treasure it or else."

A woman, giving him orders? Not just any woman. His Aella. He dropped to his knees and held out his arms from his sides. "I place my trust and my love in your hands, lass."

"You'd get better results if you placed your cock in them," Lucifer advised as he passed them, his arm draped around Gaia and squeezing an ass cheek.

"He's right. We would. What do you say we adjourn somewhere a little more private?" Aella asked.

"I know just the place." Clasping her in his arms, Niall activated his amulet and took them home. Home to his tower, and a bed.

But before he sank into the glorious heat of her body, he just had to ask, "Did ye mean it?"

He hated how needy he sounded. How unsure. Baring himself, even for the woman he loved, was hard. It seemed he wasn't the only one finding it hard to admit it aloud.

She licked her lips and swallowed, taking her time

finding the words he needed to hear. "Yes. I don't how or when it happened, but I fell in love with you. Kilt and all."

"Truly?"

"How many times do I have to say it?" She tempered her irritated retort with a stroke of her hand against his cheek. "I'll admit, I'm worried about letting you into my life. You're stuck in the dark ages and on the rebound from your first love."

Lost in her eyes, he noted for the first time a glimmer of trepidation, and he realized something shocking. His lass feared. Feared not her love for him, but the possibility that perhaps he didn't love her as much as she seemed to think he loved his past. No longer. "Despite what ye think, I never loved her. What I felt for Fionnaghal was lust, and while I did covet, it wasn't so much her I wanted as the power and prestige being her husband brought. With ye..." He trailed off and cupped her cheeks. "With ye, I don't want your land or money. I don't need power or prestige. I just want ye. I love ye, Aella. I love it when you're angry and outspoken and killing things. I love ye when ye claw my back to ribbons and scream to wake the dead. I love that ye are not meek or mild, or willing to let others make your decisions."

"Even if it does drive you mental and I need to have the last word?"

"Because ye do those things."

"So we're stuck together forever?"

"And ever."

"Seal it with a kiss?" she asked with a sensuous smile.

Her Scot did better than that. He made short work of their clothes, his powerful hands ripping them from their bodies while she laughed, a young, girlish sound, carefree and wanton.

He loved her.

Loved her despite her faults. Even because of them.

What more could she ask for?

Hmm, other than some hot sex to seal the deal. Lucky her, he had the same idea. He covered her body with his own, skin-to-skin, lips meshed, and erotic sparks sizzling between them. She arched up against him, delighting in the feel of him, the strength, the power she knew he held at bay because, for some reason, he liked to think of her as delicate. So endearing.

Maybe at another time she'd let him treat her like spun glass and an object of worship. Today, it was her turn.

"On your back," she ordered.

"When I'm done pleasuring ye." His lips teased the bud of her breast, pulling it taut and sending shivers of pleasure throughout her body.

She almost gave in. It would be so easy to let him do all the work and to bask in the climax his lips promised. But she'd rarely had a chance to explore, and she wanted to in a bad way. "Get on your back, Scot. Right now or I'll get my axe." She shoved at his solid chest, which rumbled with laughter at her threat.

"Blood-thirsty lass. It's a good thing I love ye." With a sigh of resignation, he rolled off her body onto his back.

She sat up and swallowed a sigh of her own. He was so ruggedly perfect. There he lay, waiting for her next move, his body tense with anticipation, his eyes glowing with arousal, his cock jutting upward, twitching as she stared.

"Lace your fingers under your head and keep them there," she commanded.

"Are ye about to get kinky with me?" he asked with an arched brow.

"Would you settle for dirty?"

In a blur, he did as told, and she laughed. "Now don't move." She straddled his waist, her honey-slick core resting on his muscled stomach, which clenched in response. Leaning forward, she slid her lips across his in a sensuous caress, but jerked away before he could capture her lips.

"I said don't move."

"Tease."

"You have no idea." With only her lips, she traced the edge of his unshaven jaw, nipping it lightly with her teeth. He trembled, but didn't budge. She trailed a sinuous path down his neck and, in the curve where it met his shoulder and gave him a hard suck. His body went still and stiff under hers, and the muscles in his arms strained as he fought to keep himself from moving.

She laughed as she leaned up to stare him in the eyes. How fierce he looked, his eyes glowing with an intensity she'd come to expect and love. The temptation to kiss him was strong, but she settled instead for dragging her nails over his nipples, which puckered in response. Between her nails, she pinched the tips, her thighs gripping him tightly as he bucked, his body reacting whether he wanted it to or not.

"I said stay still."

"But—"

She shushed him. "Behave, Scot, or I will make you watch as I play with myself."

"Ye are just plain evil," he said with a strained chuckle that turned into a groan as she took one of his nipples into her mouth and sucked.

"That's not evil. This is evil." She repositioned herself so that her pussy hovered over his mouth and her lips brushed the tip of his cock. A pearl formed on the head. She licked it before she slid her lips down his thick length. Then up again. Then down and up. She felt him shift, and she paused long enough to say, "Don't you dare move."

"Aella," he groaned, but he listened. Taking pity on him, she made his task easier by lowering her sex onto his mouth. He devoured her eagerly, hands still tucked under his head, but his tongue… Oh my, his tongue more than made up for it.

Distracted, she returned to her previous action of sucking. Bobbing up and down on his cock, she also cupped his balls and kneaded them until they pulled up taut.

Sixty-nine truly was the most decadent number, probably her favorite one now as they both worked the other to a fevered state. His cock swelled under her attention while he latched onto her sex with a ferocity that made her cry out, the sound vibrating around the dick in her mouth. He tongued her. Probed her. Pleasured her, bringing her to the edge.

She didn't want to fall off it without him inside her. She rolled off him, panting, and he let out a cry. "Get back here, lass. I wasn't done."

"I'm still giving the orders," she gasped. Barely.

Straddling him, her sex hovering over his cock, she lowered herself enough that the tip of his shaft nudged her lower lips. To her surprise, his hands remained laced under his head. Damn did he look sexy. She impaled herself, seating him within her, head thrown back in delight as he filled her up, stretching the walls of her channel. Once she had him firmly embedded, and throbbing within, she rocked back and forth, sending jolts of pleasure throughout her body.

"I want to touch ye," he begged.

She wiggled. "You already technically are." She smirked at his growl. Leaning forward, she grabbed his wrists, which stretched her body over his, and then she gyrated back and forth on his pelvis. It felt so fucking good as the motion ground her clit against him and drove him even deeper.

Faster. Faster.

His hips bucked, but without his hands on her hips, he got no traction. She finally relented. She released his hands. "Make me come."

Magic words. And an instant reply. His fingers dug into her as he held her in place to pound. Up he thrust, lifting and dropping her in time to his ramming. She just held on, riding him like a bucking bronco, each bounce and jounce hitting her G-spot and stimulating her throbbing clit. When she came, he yelled and pumped faster, drawing out her ecstasy, rolling her into a second climax, one that left her boneless and drowsy, enough that she collapsed atop him when he finally stilled underneath her.

He stroked the sweaty strands of her hair from her

face as he kissed her temple, then her cheek. His hands skimmed over her body as if unable to help themselves from touching.

"I love ye, lass."

"I love you too, my Scot."

"Oh, how fucking cute. Someone hand me a bucket to barf in."

Lucifer had arrived with his usual impeccable timing and laughed when Niall threatened to cut off his dick. Lying in bed, the sheet tucked around her, Aella watched as they bickered. It seemed Lucifer wanted Niall to start a golfing school. Niall refused. Lucifer threatened.

But, in the end, the devil won. Or did he? Within weeks, filled with glorious days of fucking and getting to know one another, the golfing academy was born. Niall got to play the sport he thought he hated. Aella gave up her dangerous job of tracking to take on the more hazardous one of dealing with irate students who all seemed to think they should be pro golfers after one lesson. And they lived happily ever after in a big fucking castle Niall had built for her on the edge of the sea.

It made even Zeus's wife Hera jealous. Who said you couldn't live happily ever after in Hell? Just point them out, and Aella would take care of them, with her double-edged axe.

EPILOGUE

A FEW DAYS later on the docks by the River Styx...

"You've been a bad kitty." Lucifer shook his head at the hellcat in question.

Felipe, the minion in trouble, sat on his haunches alongside his catch and hung his giant feline head, whiskers drooping.

"Don't try that innocent look with me. It might work with that witch who took you in, but it won't work with me, you rascal."

Shifting shapes until he stood as a man with his hands covering his groin, Felipe wore a sheepish expression on his face. "Would it help to say I was sorry?"

"No." Lucifer tapped his foot on the quay and shook his finger. "What have I told you about playing with the Styx monsters?"

"I was hungry."

"Then you go to the market."

"But it's not as fresh." The handsome hellcat pouted, and Lucifer fought not to smile. The shape-shifter truly had the gift of charm, and he knew it. It was why he did so well with the women, the lucky bastard.

Charon, who stood alongside watching the exchange from the dark depths of his cowl, threw up his gloved hands. "Hungry? Too fucking bad. That's the second one you've killed this month. How am I supposed to properly awe the newly damned I'm shipping across the river if we don't have any impressive specimens to scare the pants off them?"

"I think you should worry more about your son and his reputation of fucking up than my fishing habits," Felipe retorted. "Or did you not tell our lord about his latest mishap?"

Not another one. "What did Adexios do this time?" Lucifer demanded. "Did he overturn the boat again? Lose his oar?"

"I'd rather not say," Charon mumbled.

A smirk on his lips, Felipe didn't have a problem tattling. "He let one of the newly damned pilot his boat while he took a nap. The damned one immediately turned the boat around and poled it back to land."

Counting to ten didn't make the news any easier to bear, but Lucifer reined in his temper instead of blasting the bearer of the tidings into meaty chunks. "Are you trying to tell me I've got some newbies running around on the mortal plane instead of down in processing?" Given the number of souls arriving daily, Lucifer had only enough time to meet the special or most intriguing cases.

However, no one could think to accuse him of slacking on the job, even if he didn't meet or greet each damned one by name, because he ran a tight administration. Every soul that arrived got its just desserts. No bad deed went unpunished, or unapplauded.

"The good news is they're still more or less in the pit." Felipe wore a gloating grin, and Lucifer just knew he wouldn't like the rest.

"I hear a big but coming."

"They're just not within the nine circles. While Adexios snoozed, the temporary boatman dumped him and then managed to steer the boat with its passengers to Siren Isle. So the damned ones are contained. The bad news is it won't be easy getting them back." Felipe snickered as Charon groaned.

Folding his robed arms over his chest, his hands hidden in the voluminous sleeves, the full-time boatman of the Styx sighed. "I'll send my lad to get them back."

"And have him fuck something else up?" Lucifer snapped. "No, thank you. I think it's time I reassigned the boy to something a little less strenuous, and a lot less enjoyable. As for you—" Lucifer turned his mighty glare on the hellcat, who seemed entirely too pleased with himself. Time to rip the canary grin from his face. "Since you also disobeyed, don't think you're getting off scot-free. I've got a job for you. Get those souls back."

"But they're on Siren Isle."

"And?"

"Those females ensnare males and keep them as slaves."

"Then you'd better be careful."

"But—"

Drawing himself up, and letting the fires of Hell glow in his eyes— a neat trick he'd learned eons ago—Lucifer spoke. "NOW!" He might have yelled it. It sure did echo, and it had the required effect. Felipe held his cocky tongue and nodded.

Inside, Lucifer chuckled with glee. As usual, things were going along as planned. His plan. His hellcat minion was about to meet the mother of his future litters. Or get enslaved by a bunch of sirens and turned into a stud.

Either way, his will would be done.

The End (of this story)
But the fun continues…Hell's Kitty

Made in the USA
Coppell, TX
23 September 2020

38625469R00089